STARRING ME AS THIRD DONKEY

KAREN BALL

PUFFIN

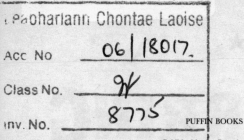
PUFFIN BOOKS

Published by the Penguin Group
Penguin Books Ltd, 80 Strand, London WC2R 0RL, England
Penguin Group (USA) Inc., 375 Hudson Street, New York, New York 10014, USA
Penguin Group (Canada), 10 Alcorn Avenue, Toronto, Ontario, Canada M4V 3B2
(a division of Pearson Penguin Canada Inc.)
Penguin Ireland, 25 St Stephen's Green, Dublin 2, Ireland (a division of Penguin Books Ltd)
Penguin Group (Australia), 250 Camberwell Road, Camberwell, Victoria 3124, Australia
(a division of Pearson Australia Group Pty Ltd)
Penguin Books India Pvt Ltd, 11 Community Centre, Panchsheel Park, New Delhi – 110 017, India
Penguin Group (NZ), cnr Airborne and Rosedale Roads, Albany, Auckland 1310, New Zealand
(a division of Pearson New Zealand Ltd)
Penguin Books (South Africa) (Pty) Ltd, 24 Sturdee Avenue, Rosebank, Johannesburg 2196, South Africa

Penguin Books Ltd, Registered Offices: 80 Strand, London WC2R 0RL, England

www.penguin.com

First published 2005
1

Set in Monotype Baskerville by
Palimpsest Book Production Limited, Polmont, Stirlingshire
Made and printed in England by Clays Ltd, St Ives plc

British Library Cataloguing in Publication Data
A CIP catalogue record for this book is available from the British Library

ISBN 0–141–31825–2

To Mum and Dad

*Thanks to Jane Burnard and Sarah, Pippa
and Lindsey at Puffin*

Prologue

Life doesn't get much better than this. I'm stuffed inside a fake-fur costume, I'm trying not to sneeze (I'm allergic to fake fur) and some sadist, otherwise known as my mum, is taking photos. Yep, when God was handing out the good times you can bet he made certain I was at the front of the queue. That's for sure.

You might be asking yourself, 'Why's Emma wearing fake fur?' I mean, it's not exactly this season's catwalk choice, is it? But you know what? I wish I *could* blame all this on a fashion mistake. At least then the fashion police would come and take me away. No. The reason I am wearing fake fur is because I am a minor character in the school's production of *Samson and Delilah*. To be more exact, I'm Third Donkey. That means that out of three very minor characters in the play – Donkey 1, Donkey 2 and Donkey 3 – I'm last in the list. The donkey no one cares about.

You see, in ye olden times they had donkeys. Apparently. So in modern times girls like me are forced to dress up as donkeys and stand onstage looking like right wallies. As you might imagine, mine isn't a large part. I'm more what you'd call decoration.

Learning my lines was humiliating. I mean, how many times do I have to practise screeching 'Eey-ore'? (Well, more times than you'd think, actually. Although Mr Taylor said he really didn't need me to make that much noise. Especially when Kate was trying to sing.)

Hold on now, here she comes. Enter stage right, ready to launch into another awful song. My best friend, Kate. Or should I say Delilah: the star of the stage, princess for a night, hair-dresser to the biblical. That's right. That one there in the thick, black eyeliner and well-dodgy wig. My best friend is the star turn in *Samson and Delilah – the musical.* I ask you. What the heck did Old Testament characters have to sing about anyway?

You're probably wondering how I managed

to get involved in all this in the first place. Unfortunately, there's only one person to blame. Me. I can't blame school and I can't even blame my parents. I actually volunteered – not to be a donkey, don't get me wrong. Let's just say that my grand Oscar ambitions didn't quite hit their target.

CHAPTER ONE

So there are these two girls, Kate and Emma. We've loads of attitude. You can tell that by the way we each stand with a skinny hip cocked out, ignoring each other and everyone around us. We're the ace supremos of cool and we're constantly in demand. Pop stars, super-models, world-famous actors . . . they're always asking, 'How do those girls *do* that?' Our teachers seem to understand when we have to miss school for the Oscar ceremonies each year. After all, you can't say 'No' to Hollywood.

Hmm, well, maybe that's not exactly how it is. OK, so here's the truth: Kate's the kind of girl everyone loves. Ms Popularity with a capital 'P'. And then there's Emma (that's me). I suffer the curse of being normal, whereas Kate is blessed with having Something Special.

All the younger kids at school follow her around the playground in this worshipful way and, quite frankly, it's hard work being Kate's best friend. You're constantly reminded how great she is. Every day I have to listen to any of the following:

'Well done, Kate! Another excellent essay.'

'Would you like some of my sandwiches?'

'Can I be in Kate's team?'

'And the winner is . . . Kate Hardcastle.'

Do you see what I mean?

Well, it would be hard work being Kate's friend if I didn't *like* her so much. You don't have much choice with Kate – the rest of us are like iron filings round a magnet. She's everything we would all like to be – clever and pretty, and kind and talented. But we know we'll never be *that* great. So we settle for the next best thing. We settle for being near Kate. Which means Kate should be the most spoilt prima donna ever to walk this earth, right? Well, wrong. Kate hasn't let it all go to her head. She's clearly some kind of superhuman being. And not only is she a superhuman being, she's my friend. 'Which,' Kate always says, 'makes me a double super-human being.' Then the two of us settle together in our place on the school steps – third step up, one bum space away from the crack in the concrete where Mr Key dropped the sports trophy two summers ago.

'I hereby announce the opening of the second annual meeting of the Kate Fan Club,' I declare pompously. 'First item on the agenda, What Makes Kate So Perfect?' Then we both pretend to stick our fingers down our throats and throw up.

You see, that's why we work so well together. Kate doesn't take herself too seriously and neither do I. I know Kate better than anybody – I've seen her pick her scabs when she thought her mum wasn't looking, and I've seen her cry like a baby when she's frightened herself diving off the top board in the swimming pool. I know Kate Hardcastle isn't so perfect. And Kate knows I know and she likes that. I keep her feet on the ground.

And that's pretty much how it all was the day that the school play was announced. Mr Key was taking morning assembly and we were all picking our noses. As you do. Then, just as we thought he had spluttered to an end he took us all by surprise.

'And finally, I'm very pleased to announce that this year's school play will be *Samson and Delilah – the musical*. Hands up anyone who can tell me who Samson and Delilah were.' He looked at us hopefully.

Thundering silence.

I mean, even if we did know, we weren't about to admit it in front of the whole school, were we? Peter nudged me, pretending to encourage me to put my hand up. I nudged him back silently and was pleased to see him wince in pain as my elbow made contact with his ribs. We grinned at each other. I'd been friends with Peter for almost as long as I could remember, and I knew I'd have to go pretty far to make him want to fall out with me. As Second Best Friends went, Peter was as good as it gets.

'Well,' cough, cough, 'don't worry. You'll all be learning about the story of these two characters in the next few weeks. Mr Taylor has kindly volunteered to direct the play and he'll be holding auditions at the end of this week. So for all you budding actors and actresses out there – here's your chance to tread the boards!'

As we trailed out of the assembly hall there was a buzz of excitement. Well, if you listened very hard you could just about make out a buzz. Admittedly, hardly any of us knew anything about this Samson bloke and his girlfriend, Delilah. But I had to admit, I was interested in finding out more. Whoever Delilah was, with a name like that she had to be pretty glamorous. The only problem was, everyone in our entire school wanted to be an actor or a pop star. We'd watched the reality TV shows and knew all you needed to find overnight super-stardom was a loud voice and a lot of cheek. The competition was going to be tough.

'Do you reckon you might have a go? Turn up to auditions, like?' I asked Kate, trying to sound like I wasn't bothered. I wasn't sure if it was cool or not to sound interested in the play. Also, I knew I'd need all the extra rehearsal time I could lay my hands on to get ready for auditions – if I was going to take part. And it was a big IF.

'Well, I might not be right for the part,' Kate said in a bored voice. 'And I'm not even sure I can fit it in, what with ballet practice and just starting my cello lessons, then there's yoga on a Saturday morning . . .'

'Yeah. I suppose it would be a bit of a drag volunteering for a stupid school play,' I agreed, my secret hopes of stardom fading. But then I noticed Kate's cheeky grin.

'Oh, Emma, don't be silly! I was only joking. This is brilliant! We'll have such a laugh!'

'Really? I mean, I can see you in it. But . . . both of us?' I asked uncertainly.

'Of course, both of us! We've got to be in this play together,' she replied excitedly. A couple of boys wandered past, nudging each other and sniggering, but they may as well have been on another planet for all we cared. Kate's excitement was catching and let's face it – I didn't really need that much persuading. We gripped each other's arms and jumped up and down on the spot.

'The two of us!' I cheered.

'Together!' she agreed.

'To your classrooms!' Mr Key interrupted.

We swivelled round to see our headmaster standing behind us. He gave us a fat wink to let us know he was only teasing. 'Glad to see you're both so keen,' he said, scrabbling in the tiny pocket of his waistcoat until he managed to pull out the fob watch he kept there. 'But you're still seven minutes late, girls.'

I can't say it was up there in the Top Ten Most Terrifying Tellings-Off we'd ever had. Still, with good grace we started to back away from him towards our classroom, when suddenly Mr Key looked up, strode towards us and leant in so closely that I was shoved out of the way by his scratchy, stiff tweed elbow. I could see it wasn't me he wanted to speak to.

'Now, Kate, dear, I know you've a talent for drama and I don't want to give too much away at this point,' he stage-whispered. 'But we've already had a few informal chats in the staffroom and we all know you were born to play Delilah. Especially Mr Taylor,' he added. And with that he smoothed down his waistcoat and shuffled off.

Kate and I raised our eyebrows at each other in the way that only Kate and I know about. It's what we always did when someone started to gush over Kate. Neither one of us was impressed by the way strangers, friends and even teachers thought that Kate was just too brilliant for words.

'It's a shame, really,' Kate would comment, pulling a thick strand of pink bubble-gum from between her teeth and twirling it round her forefinger. 'They're setting themselves up for disappointment . . .'

'Too right,' I'd agree, watching with fascination as my apparently perfect best friend managed to twirl bubblegum all over herself. 'Especially when they find out about your disgusting eating habits.' And then we'd shrug a synchronized bemused shrug.

But this morning felt different. As Mr Key retreated into his office, I couldn't help rubbing my arm where our headmaster had elbowed me out of the way, feeling hurt that he hadn't said anything to encourage *me* up on to the stage.

☆☆☆

'Well!' our teacher, Miss Cameron, exclaimed. 'I think in the light of this morning's announcement, we really must take a look at Samson and Delilah, don't you?' Miss Cameron prides herself on being a bit alternative. She doesn't like teaching lessons the straightforward way. She says she likes to 'bring subjects to life' in her lessons. Between you and me, Miss Cameron should know better. It was a pretty painful performance that morning. But we liked her, so we did our best to look interested.

'All right, everybody, pay attention; Peter, put that compass down and, Emma, stop chatting, please. OK, Samson and Delilah. Now you're probably thinking, "Oh, the Bible, it's full of fuddy-duddy old people who wear tea towels on their heads," aren't you? Well, you know, Samson and Delilah were a pretty cool couple, actually. I mean, they're a bit like – oh, what's that couple, you know the pop star and the footballer – Nosh and Pecs. Yes, really! Admittedly, Delilah was pretty good at singing. But just like Nosh she knew how to get her man. She used her feminine wiles.

No, Peter, I am not going to explain feminine wiles, work it out for yourself. And Samson – well, Samson's heart was in the right place but he didn't have enough up top to see through Delilah's schemes. So he was a lot like Pecs – a sportsman of great ability but don't rely on him to work out the cost of the groceries. Are you keeping up?'

And on and on. We didn't have a clue what Miss Cameron was talking about. Nikky leant across from her desk and twirled a finger round by the side of her head, implying that Miss Cameron had lost it. Kate tried to look disapproving, but neither of us could resist laughing.

It's always best to laugh when Nikky cracks a joke anyway. She looks hard as nails – and, rumour has it, she is. Stare gormlessly in her direction if you dare, because she'll waste no time in starting a fight. And if you can't fight, she'll look at you in disgust, punch you on the shoulder and ask if you fancy a game of British Bulldog with her and the boys from the big school. But despite all of this, we couldn't help loving Nikky. School's like that, isn't it? One day you're struggling to learn how to count to ten together, the next thing you know you've all become obsessed with *Pop Idol*, and some of these characters you're forced to spend five days a week with have turned into friends.

Nikky didn't exactly grow on us, more punched us in the face with the full force of her personality. She came to our school late – just turned up one morning in the middle of term. Of course, by that stage, we'd already formed our little groups. Everyone had a best friend, and it must have been pretty scary to be standing in the middle of a classroom of strangers and not a best friend in sight. But that seemed to make no difference at all. Nikky stood with her feet apart, legs braced, in a grubby T-shirt and carrying an older brother's discarded backpack, and she looked . . . well, she looked superior to the rest of us. Like a conquering gladiator (just without the leather armour and sword). You couldn't help being awestruck. And when Miss Cameron asked her what her name was, such a big voice came out of that skinny little frame: 'Nikky, Miss.' You couldn't believe that someone, especially a new person, could speak like that. But Nikky did. Nikky wasn't scared of anything. And before I knew what I was doing, I was pulling a chair out and inviting Nikky to sit down next to Kate and me.

'What's that, Nikky?' Miss Cameron suddenly demanded, swivelling on a heel.

'Incredible,' murmured Nikky under her breath. 'They really do have eyes in the back of their heads.' Then louder for Miss Cameron's benefit: 'I was just wondering if there's something about this in the *Illustrated Bible*, Miss Cameron.' Our teacher didn't look convinced, but she decided not to make a fuss, satisfying herself instead by dropping the Bible with a loud thump on to Nikky's desk. The rest of us gathered round.

THE CHILDREN'S ILLUSTRATED BIBLE

The Story of Samson and Delilah

Samson was a Nazirite, set apart for God's service. As part of his calling, he could not cut off his hair or drink alcohol. He was an extremely strong man, who could tear a lion apart with his bare hands.

A Philistine woman, called Delilah, was instructed to find out the source of Samson's strength. If she managed to solve the mystery, she'd be paid a lot of money. She nagged and nagged him, and asked how Samson could truly love her if he wouldn't tell her his secret. Eventually, Samson gave in and told Delilah the reason for his strength – his hair. It had never been cut. He told her, 'If my head was shaved, my strength would leave me, and I would become as weak as any other man.'

That night Delilah betrayed Samson. He fell asleep in Delilah's lap and she cut off his hair.

The Philistines woke him roughly, gouged out his eyes, chained him up and put him in prison. But what the Philistines forgot is that Samson's hair would grow out again. Slowly and secretly, Samson was regaining his strength.

One day he was allowed out of prison so that the Philistines could gloat over their prisoner. They stood Samson among the pillars, and he rested his hands on them as though he were weak and tired. Then Samson prayed to the Lord for strength and braced himself against the pillars. He pushed with all his might and the temple came clattering down on the rulers and people – and Samson himself.

Everyone had something to say.

'What kind of idiot thinks long hair makes him strong?'

'Well, what about those WWF wrestlers? They all have long hair.'

'And what's with all the stuff about nagging? Those Bible writers were so sexist!' (Nikky was always being told by her mum that women were equal to men, even if mums did seem to do most of the cooking and the cleaning. And Nikky never failed to pass the same message on to us.)

'So, what? We're saying Delilah is more like that maths woman off *Countdown*?'

'Totally! That Samson was just a big girl with long hair. He deserved everything he got!'

Miss Cameron had turned round from the whiteboard and was beaming all over her face.

'Excellent! Excellent! I can see I've lit a touchpaper. You're really getting the hang of this. And, Nikky, well done for bringing a feminist analysis to the story. You're quite right, we must never take for granted anything we read about women in the Bible or anywhere else for that matter.'

The rest of the lesson was devoted to a

passionate debate on the subject. By the end of class we'd agreed that Delilah was a clever girl, but she probably did rely a bit too much on her heaving bosoms to finish Samson off. Although I'm sure half the class didn't know a heaving bosom from the school hamster.

But you could tell Kate's mind was elsewhere. She hardly contributed at all and when Miss Cameron asked what she thought, Kate just said, 'Oh, well. I agree with Emma.' And I hadn't even said anything! Yep, Kate definitely had her sights set on something grander than being an RE debating star. That girl had sniffed the greasepaint and she wasn't auditioning for the fun of it. My friend meant business.

The problem was, so did I. After the tiniest bit of encouragement from my best friend, and despite Mr Key totally ignoring me, I was desperate to take my place on that rickety stage. And not just in any old part. I wanted centre-stage stardom and a big golden star on my dressing-room door, a silk dressing gown to wear in my dressing room and beautiful flowers delivered by fawning admirers. The only part that would give me that kind of superstardom was the main female lead: Delilah. The only flaw in my otherwise flawless plan was I knew that Kate, a naturally talented actress with a pretty face, would be perfect in that role. I mean perfect. Would she be happy to step aside all martyr-like and let someone else take the main part? I didn't think so.

This was strange. It wasn't in my nature to get excited about things. I was usually too busy taking the mickey. But I'll be honest with you, I was tired of hiding behind smart-alec comments to get through life, school and existence in general. I just wanted to do something interesting and not have to worry what people thought for a change. Of course, I should have known better. I should have listened to my instincts and left well enough alone. But no. With auditions at the end of the week, in a few days from now I was going to make a complete ass of myself. Literally.

CHAPTER TWO

The reality of the school play didn't really kick in that day until I got home after school. Now, home is where most people go for a bit of peace and quiet in front of the telly. But with me, it's the other way round. I'm one of the few people who like going to school . . . just to get away from the chaos at home. With a baby brother in the house and an actress for a mother, there's always a drama waiting to unfold. And you may not know this, but actresses don't do housework. Not according to my mum. I've tried telling her how embarrassing she is and that my life has been ruined forever by her inability to use an iron, but my mum sighs in a world-weary way and says, 'Well, darling, that's what mums are for. We take the blame for everything.'

You see, my mum just isn't like other mums. And when you're my age, you don't need anyone showing you up. She says she's . . . what's the word she uses? . . . 'bourgeoise'. Well, whatever that word means, as far as I can see, in my mum's case it means you don't get your hair cut as often as you should and you're always banging on about 'Plays I Once Shone In'. Yes, she's a bit of an actress, my mum. And because she's an actress, this means she treats even the smallest occasion as an opportunity to show off.

Let me give you an example. Most kids my age get to go to bed without much of a fuss, right? I mean, in the part of the world where I come from, most parents think that shows of affection are the kind of thing that ruins a child. Frankly, I agree with them. Unfortunately for me, my mum does not. She likes to 'Emote'. (That's an acting term for showing off.)

So, as I was saying, getting to bed is a bit of a chore. First of all my mum has to wrap me up in a big bear hug as though she's never going to see me ever again, and then she runs through her tick list of endearments: 'Oh, darling, sweetheart, pussycat, light of my life, child of my loins . . . give me a kiss goodnight.'

And that's *without* an audience! But allow her out among the wider public and, honestly, the woman is a walking liability. Dad and I were becoming seriously worried at one point. 'I'm very concerned, Emma,' Dad confided to me one evening when we were pretending to play French cricket up on the playing fields. (Neither of us likes sport much, but apparently this is the kind of thing Mum thinks dads and daughters are meant to do together. It helps us bond, apparently. There you go – that emotion stuff again.) Dad gazed forlornly after two boys from the estate who had run off with our cricket bat.

'What is it?' I asked, though I had a good idea what the problem was.

'It's your mother,' he said guiltily. 'My boss has stopped inviting us to dinner, and Derek from Accounts says it's because your mum can't stop taking over the conversation. It's the wine, you know,' Dad continued, adjusting the tracksuit bottoms Mum had forced him to wear. 'Give her one glass of it and it's *A Midsummer Night's Dream* all over again. Even when it's January.'

Fortunately for my dad, I'd been doing some research of my own by that time, spurred on by experiencing one too many of Mum's embarrassing recitals myself.

'I've got an idea,' I said as the two of us walked home together that evening, resigned to never seeing our cricket bat again.

'What is it?' Dad asked, a flicker of desperate hope lighting up his eyes. I pulled a pink flyer out of my jeans pocket and held it out in front of him.

'*Look!*' I said, feeling smug already.

Dad opened the crumpled sheet of paper and squinted, holding the flyer out at arm's length. No wonder he couldn't throw a ball. 'Amateur dramatics. New members needed for the forthcoming production of . . .' Dad paused and looked down at me.

I nodded for him to continue.

'*A Midsummer Night's Dream*!' he exclaimed loudly.

'What's that you said?' Mum's head appeared out of an upstairs window.

Dad looked up at her uncertainly. 'She might not like the "amateur" bit,' he whispered to me.

'She'll love it,' I said confidently. 'She'll be able to tell all the others what to do.'

That clinched it.

'Mary!' Dad called up to the open window. 'How do you fancy playing Titania?'

And that was that. Mum found her outlet and Dad got his promotion. It didn't stop Mum being high maintenance, but it did keep Dad and me relatively sane; after that we could just about put up with the chaos at home. Just.

Today was typical. I got home, kicked the door shut and dropped my school bag on the floor. I waited for Mum to tell me to pick it up again, but no such luck. She didn't even notice. In fact, she probably approves of behaviour like that. Instead, she grabbed me from left field and gave me a big kiss. It was pretty uncomfortable, what with Sam stuck between the two of us like the filling in a baby sandwich. He's only six months old and he's probably already scarred for life.

Our conversation went like this:

'How was school today?'

'Eunghh.'

'Excellent! Did anything interesting happen?'

'Mnphhh.'

'So, you weren't there when Mr Key announced the school play then?'

'HOW DO YOU KNOW ABOUT THAT?'

I couldn't believe it. Is this what it had come to? My mum sending spies into the school?

'Have you been sending spies into school?' I demanded.

'Don't be silly, sweetness. Kate's mum phoned and she told me all about it. It sounds wonderful! I think you should definitely go to the auditions, it'll do you the world of good.'

Of course, I should have anticipated this.

Kate and I have the same walk to school, but Kate's street turns off to the right just where the big conker tree cranes out over the corner of Church Lane and I have to walk the last five minutes home on my own. (And it is only five minutes, certainly no longer, because my mum, as local drama queen, decides that I have been chopped to pieces by a mass murderer if I don't walk through the front door punctually just as *Countdown* is finishing.) Kate must have told her mum as soon as she got home, which means that her mum must have dialled in double quick time, talked at superspeed down the phone and possibly not even allowed my mum to interrupt her (which is no mean feat, let me tell you). All before I'd even got through the front door. Impressive, but worrying. There were far too many people getting far too excited for my liking. It made me nervous.

'She didn't waste much time,' I commented grumpily, but Mum didn't take any notice. She was too busy holding my baby brother's bum up to her face and sniffing his nappy. 'Disgusting,' I hissed, in a pathetic attempt to take my bad mood out on someone else. I've found it's a good rule to have in life: when you're feeling pants, make someone else feel the same way. It makes them much more sympathetic. Not.

Mum wandered off up the stairs, holding Sam at arm's length. I sank on to the sofa and began picking the latest scab to adorn my knee. Scab-picking is always good to do when you need to think carefully about something. It was obvious that Kate was taking this play *way* seriously. Serious enough to think about the role of Delilah. And she was excited. Which meant she had to believe that she had a strong chance of winning the lead part. That's the only thing that could explain why she was volunteering school news to her mum. And I couldn't help wondering that if Kate was excited, where did that leave me?

'Hope' is a dangerous word. Add an 'l' and an 'e' and a double 's', and that was a pretty accurate description of my chances of getting the star role in the play. But during those last five minutes of this afternoon's walk home from school, those five minutes when Kate and Kate's mum and my mum were all gabbing away to each other, I hadn't felt grumpy at all for a change. I'd started to let myself hope that I could . . . I might . . . I mean . . . could I? Be Delilah?

But walking through the front door had brought me back down to earth with a bump. Just listening to my mum wittering on about the play was enough to make my palms go hot and sticky. I didn't know if I dared admit to her or anybody that I wanted to go for it. I looked down at my knee to discover that I'd managed to pick my scab so that it had stopped looking like a map of the United States and had become a very rough outline of Italy. Things were getting out of control.

I pulled my mobile phone out of my

backpack and looked at the screen to see if any text messages were waiting for me. There was just one from Peter asking if I'd had my tea yet, but that was only so that he could have a good laugh at my expense. My mum should be jailed for cruelty to food. And cruelty to her children for making me eat that stuff. I started to send a text message to Kate, but then ran out of patience with the side of my thumb refusing to hit the right keys, so I decided to phone her instead.

'Hiya, Emma,' Kate said amiably.

'You told your mum, then?' I asked in a pretending-to-be-bored type of way. But the phone threatened to slip from my grip because of the hot, sticky palm thing that was still happening, and I took my hand away, craning my neck as the phone perched between the side of my face and my shoulder. It's not the most comfortable way of talking to someone.

'Oh yeah, sorry about that. Typical mums, can't keep off the phone from each other. She didn't spoil things for you, did she?'

'What do you mean?' I asked.

'I mean, you know. You might have been looking forward to telling your mum yourself.' Kate said reasonably.

But that would have involved admitting I am excited, which would have involved admitting I am nervous, which would have involved admitting I even think I have a chance as Delilah, I felt like saying. But I didn't. For one thing, I don't think I'd have had the breath in my body to get out a sentence that long. I didn't say anything.

'Emma?' Kate asked. 'You still there?'

'Mmmm,' I mumbled down the phone. 'Listen. Can we try to keep this whole play thing a bit low-key? You know what my mum is like. I don't want her getting overexcited. It won't do me any good at all.'

'Understood,' Kate agreed. 'I am sorry. Perhaps I'll cut the phone wires here and then my mum won't be able to phone your mum any more.'

'I think that's why they invented mobiles,' I said. 'Mobiles are a mum secret weapon so that they can keep in touch at all times.'

'And we thought they were invented so that kids could play *Snake II*,' Kate said sadly.

'Don't you believe it,' I warned. 'It's all part

of the conspiracy.' We agreed to meet outside the park the next morning and hung up.

Now I know what you're thinking. You're thinking, 'So if Emma is such good friends with Kate, why doesn't she just tell her about the hot, sticky palm thing?' And I can see why. Kate has known me for approximately six zillion years (which is a pretty long time when you consider that we haven't even done our GCSEs yet). She knows that getting panicked about a lot of things in life is what I do best.

And when I get my knickers in a twist, Kate knows exactly what to do. She must spend approximately half her life helping me to calm down. A reassuring squeeze of my arm, a whispered answer in class, a shove in the back when I need to step forward. Most people don't ever see these things, but a million of these tiny gestures from Kate have stopped me from being the biggest drama queen since, well, my mum.

But the problem is that you end up feeling a burden. And guilty. So a lot of the time, I can't tell Kate what's bugging me. I just have to wait for her to work it out. Because if I ever actually came out with it and told her straight . . . well, that's the moment I would have to admit that without a Kate Hardcastle hanging around, I would be in a lot of trouble. And no one wants to admit that the only reason they can cope is because of someone else. There was a lot out there waiting for us: big school, university, jobs . . . I couldn't exactly picture Kate still holding my hand when I was wearing a suit, in the middle of a management meeting, giving a deal-making presentation to the board. 'Don't mind my friend,' I'd say as I walked towards the flip chart at the top of the meeting room, Kate smiling at all the fat men in grey suits and whispering, 'Just pretend I'm not here.' I don't think so.

But anyway, that was all in the future. I could worry about that any time. My most immediate and pressing problem was what I was going to do about the play. If I didn't even dare *talk* about this play to anyone, then how was I ever going to get through an audition? And even if I did, and Mr Taylor actually offered me a part, never mind the lead role, how would I be able to get up on stage? At all?

So, obviously – I should just not do anything. I'd tell Kate tomorrow that I'd changed my mind. That was definitely the safest thing to do. Wasn't it? But even as I wandered through to the pantry to find the first-aid kit for a plaster for the Italy-shaped scab, I knew that it was too late. I'd gone and let myself hope and now there was no getting away from the fact that, like it or not, Delilah or not, Kate or not, I just had to see a copy of that script. I felt sick with hope and panic. It was almost enough to put a girl off her tea. I said *almost*. No, what really puts a girl off her tea is my mum's cooking.

Dad arrived home from work a couple of hours later and, as usual, Mum had to rush to lay the table before he covered it with his papers. 'Emma!' Mum hollered. 'Tea's up! Your favourite – cold salad.' I hauled myself off the sofa and dragged my feet towards the travesty I knew was waiting for me. Dad was already shovelling coleslaw into his mouth. He almost looked as though he didn't mind.

'Emma! Your mum's told me about the school play. What a turn-up for the books, eh? You'd do a smashing job, I can't wait to see you belt out a few numbers.'

We already had one actress in the house,

so I couldn't work out why my dad was so enthusiastic.

'What makes you think I'm going to audition?' I asked, spearing a lettuce leaf and looking at it in disgust. Yes, there was a note of stroppiness in my voice, I'll admit it. But heck, if you've got two parents available for exploitation, it would be rude not to take your bad mood out on both of them.

'Now then, love. Don't get all defensive. Your mum and I think you'd really enjoy doing a spot of acting. And it'd do you the world of good.' He stabbed a pickled onion with his fork and bit into it, crunching loudly.

I sniffed derisively.

Dad cleared his throat.

I narrowed my eyes and Dad shifted nervously in his seat. But just then Mum jumped in.

'Emma, darling . . .' she wheedled.

'Yes?' I asked, gazing at my boiled egg resignedly as it slowly turned pink from the pickled beetroot. Here it came.

'Why don't I come in to see Mr Taylor tomorrow, and we can chat about your chances of taking one of the main parts in the play?'

I stared accusingly at her. This was even worse than I expected.

'Are you saying you want a quiet word in Mr Taylor's ear? Are you trying to exert undue influence on the decision-making process, Mum?'

Mum turned a satisfying shade of pink.

'Darling, what are you saying? Shush yourself. I never thought any such thing. My God, do you think I can't remember how difficult auditions are? It's just that it might help if you knew someone was on your side.'

'Auditions Are The Great Leveller. That's what you always told me, Mum. Talent Will Out.'

'That's right!' Mum interrupted, looking flustered.

'So if you go to see Mr Taylor, that means either you're an interfering mother . . .' I paused, struggling to mask the look of triumph that was threatening to break out over my face. 'Or you don't think I've got the talent.' Mum took turns at looking horrified, disappointed and hurt. None of it disguised her embarrassment.

'Oh, Emma. All I'm trying to do is help. I've experienced the joys of the stage and I just want you to have the same.' She quickly began to forget her embarrassment and started to get that faraway look in her eyes. 'Oh, the smell of the greasepaint, the roar of the crowd, the . . .'

This was my moment to escape. Nodding and smiling encouragingly, I slowly slid from my chair and backed out of the room. Dad was already hiding behind the newspaper so I was able to make a clear getaway and hotfoot it to my bedroom. As I trotted up the stairs I could still hear her. 'They said I was another Vivien Leigh . . .'

I sat up in bed that night with my book in front of me, but I wasn't really reading anything. I was in a mild state of self-induced panic, helped along by a big dose of terror. But you wouldn't know it to look at me as Dad came in and murmured, 'Night, love,' kissing the top of my head with Sam dangling from his grasp, trying to put his fingers up my nostrils. Neither of them noticed my near-hysterical state as I turned a page and snuggled deeper beneath the quilt. Families are like that – can't see what's right in front of their eyes unless it's someone saying, 'Please would you take this million squid off me, I'm bored with it?'

I was terrified. After my dinner-table performance it was clear that the greasepaint gene was in my blood. And OK, I had the gene, but did I have the guts? Putting myself up on stage? That was no laughing matter. Still, whatever I'd said to my mum and dad, I did want to audition. Badly.

I'd fallen for the role of Delilah as soon as I'd heard her exotic name. But without some serious help getting over my fear of the stage I wouldn't get on to the celebrity D-list, never mind become an A-list star of the show. I vowed to speak to Kate first thing the next morning. Despite my worries about being a burden, I knew she was the only one who could get me through the audition. Whether I liked it or not, Kate would have to help me one more time. I put down my book and switched off the light. Sweet dreams? Biblical nightmares, more like.

CHAPTER THREE

The next morning I waited for Kate, as agreed, in our usual place at our usual time. I leant back against the park railings and lazily watched Mrs Brown from down the road appear on cue, walking her dog past the swings. The overweight Labrador pulled back on his leash as he always did, begging to be allowed to return home, until with the customary yank Mrs Brown persuaded him to take one last stroll round the park.

I sighed and looked down at my watch. Everything was as it always was every morning, but Kate was late. I poked at my backpack with the tip of my shoe so that it fell open and I reached inside for my mobile phone. I'd already checked twice and knew there were no text messages waiting for me. But I looked again, just to make sure. As I raised my head and screwed my eyes up against the early morning sunshine, a straggle of boys appeared on the horizon. They were shouting and laughing among themselves, shoving each other and turning round to check out the couple who followed close behind. I squinted a bit more. The girl seemed vaguely familiar to me, but as I tried to get a better look, my phone let out a short, polyphonic blast of a pop song to let me know a text message had arrived. 'Finally,' I grumbled to myself as I opened the text message. I knew it would be from Kate.

Oops, soz! C U @ skool. Slept in.

I sighed and slung my backpack over my shoulder.

'All alone today?' asked Mrs Brown as the Labrador threw her a resentful glance before collapsing in a heap.

'Looks like it,' I replied glumly before setting off to school by myself.

☆ ☆ ☆

'Whaddya mean, Gloria looks like a bimbo? Huh? Are you suggesting that just because a girl wears glitter nail varnish she can't use her brain? I'd be very careful, mister.'

I could hear Nikky before I'd even walked into the playground. But even I was impressed when I turned in through the school gates and found her poking her finger at an older boy. And he looked like he was about to burst into tears.

I grabbed Nikky by the collar and dragged her away from the boy, who was now struggling to compose himself. 'Calm down, Nikky! It's too early in the morning. Break us in gently, won't you?' She shrugged me off and threw a final scowl over her shoulder at him.

'Have you seen Kate?' I asked. Nikky shook her head. For some reason, I wasn't convinced by Kate's sleeping-in story. Kate was so perfect in every other aspect of her life, I couldn't imagine her doing something as devil-may-care as ignoring the alarm clock. Just then Nikky went off on one again.

'Phew-ee, check it out. Kate's gone and got herself *another* new fan club.'

And suddenly there she was. The sun was

behind her and gave all her edges a fuzzy look, like you see in the films when the woman runs across the field in slow motion – just before falling in a cowpat. The blonde wisps of Kate's hair caught the sunshine and formed a halo round her head as she walked up the playground towards us.

'She's born to be biblical,' I whispered to myself, not realizing I was talking out loud.

'What's that?' Nikky asked, looking at me strangely.

'Nothing,' I said, pushing her away as she tried to peer into my face.

I turned back to my friend who, I now noticed, was encircled by some boys I thought I recognized. They were all jostling each other, trying to pull Kate's long, blonde ponytail – in that juvenile way boys do. Kate should have looked irritated by this, but even though she ducked her head, she blushed and smiled despite herself. Eventually, one of the boys broke away from the crowd and the group dissolved from round Kate as all his mates chased after the boy up the playground.

As Kate approached, Nikky nudged me and

whispered, 'Go on, you idiot. You're the one who's so keen to know where she's been!'

'Kate?' I asked. 'Are you OK? What was that all about?' I watched in bemusement as Kate's face changed from a pale white to a pretty unappealing salmon-pink colour. I couldn't work out what was wrong with her. I blundered on. 'Well? Where have you been?' A couple of lads sauntered past – stragglers from the gang – and Kate's pink face turned red.

'Oh, you know. Just couldn't get out of bed this morning . . .' Then she faked a yawn. You always know when a yawn isn't real, because you don't want to yawn along with the person. And I definitely was not feeling any yawning coming on. I had a sneaking suspicion that there was something Kate wasn't telling me, but I hadn't any time to prise a confession out of her.

'Oh well, good job you're here now. I want to talk to you about the school play. You've got to help me audition, Kate, it's imperative. I mean, I know this is all meant to be a Big Laugh and everything but we have a serious problem here, because I don't know what the heck I'm doing and your mum's phoned my mum and now my mum's gone and got all excited. You know what she's like. She thinks she's Dame Judy Dench and she's determined I'm going to be the next Kate Winslet. I'm telling you, I need your help.' It all came out in one long gulp of a sentence.

Kate looked at me in amusement. She stuck her arm in mine and marched me towards the school steps while indicating to Nikky with a jerk of her head that she should make herself disappear for a while. Nikky looked like she wanted to argue the point, but spotted a group of boys on the other side of the playground to challenge to a fight. She ran off.

Kate and I sat down on the school steps – the place we always settled for our morning snack. Kate pulled a strawberry shoelace out of her pocket and silently passed it to me, then dragged out one for herself and dangled it into her mouth. She chewed it contemplatively, staring into the middle distance.

'What are you doing, Emma?' she asked.

'Erm, eating this sweet you just gave me?' I suggested.

'As well as that . . .' she prompted. I tried to pretend I didn't know what she was talking about. Kate prised a dusty Cheese String out of her other pocket and turned to look at me. 'You're getting all worked up again, aren't you?' she said, waving the Cheese String in my face to emphasize each word. She paused to take a bite as I nodded dumbly. 'OK, well, look. You need to calm down. What about some *pranayama*?'

'I knew those yoga lessons were a mistake,' I said grumpily as I watched Kate clear our backpacks out of the way. Although, actually, I had already started to cheer up. Two months ago Kate had forced me to sign up for some Saturday morning yoga lessons with her. 'Oh, darling,' my mum had said when I'd asked her for the registration money. 'I always knew you had a bit of Buddha in you.' And she began chanting. But as far as I was concerned, all this meditation and yoga stuff was embarrassing. Why couldn't we just go to the swimming club and get verrucas, like everyone else? But Kate had been determined. And Kate had been right. Despite myself, I'd started to enjoy yoga. It was only a bit of stretching after all.

'Come *on*,' said Kate, patting the ground next to her where she sat cross-legged. I slid across and the two of us looked round the playground to make sure the coast was clear. Most of the other kids had already made their way to the classrooms. We straightened our backs, just like Kate's mum had shown us. (Oh, I forgot to mention. Kate's mum happens to be the yoga teacher. She's a black belt in yoga – or she would be, except I don't think yoga teachers encourage karate-chop-type violence.) We breathed deeply in and out through our noses, with our hands resting on our knees, each of us sneaking a peep at the other even though our eyes were meant to be shut.

It kind of worked. I was so busy feeling foolish that I forgot I was feeling panicked. Finally, one of the older boys walked past and threw an old tennis ball at us. 'Idiots!' he said.

'Just because you're not in touch with your inner self!' Kate called after him.

'I am so,' he called back. 'He phoned only last night and said it's really nice down in Bridlington this time of year.'

As he disappeared through the school doors Kate and I looked at each other and laughed.

'Better?' she asked, pulling me to my feet.

'Better,' I agreed, dusting off the back of my skirt. 'But you will help me with the play, won't you?'

'Course I will. What are best friends for?' Kate said, looking at her watch. The morning bell rang out just as we stepped into the corridor.

'Come on!' I said, and the two of us broke into a run.

AUDITIONS ON FRIDAY, 10 a.m. SHARP! CAST MEMBERS NEEDED! PICK UP COPIES OF THE SCRIPT FROM MR TAYLOR.

```
Cast list:
God
Samson
Delilah
Delilah's mum
Samson's dad
Samson's mum
Friend of Samson 1
Friend of Samson 2
Priest 1
Priest 2
Innkeeper
```

```
Nazirites(unspecified number)
Philistines(unspecified
   number)
Plebians(unspecified
   number)
Donkey 1
Donkey 2
Donkey 3
Ox 1
Ox 2
Choir
```

We will also need members of the choir
to learn songs and attend rehearsals.
Those of you who are tone-deaf — please
stay away. Yes, that means you, Andrew
McGee.

Peter, Nikky, Kate and I crowded round the
notice. None of us said a word, but we were
all thinking the same thing.

Finally, Peter let out a long, low whistle. 'I
can't believe it,' he said. 'That is some serious
casting. The man himself's in our play.'

'I know,' said Nikky. 'Who on earth are they
going to cast as God?' Then she suddenly
stopped picking at the edge of the temporary

tattoo on her arm and looked back at the noticeboard, her face alight with inspiration. 'Of course, it's so obvious. Me! They've got to give me that role. I dare them to say God can't wear a skirt!'

She was right, it *was* perfect. Nikky had found the role of her life. And we certainly weren't about to start arguing with her. We didn't have time. She ran off down the corridor, cackling with delight, teachers ducking for cover.

The rest of us turned back to the noticeboard. 'I think I'll go for one of the plebians,' Peter said, as though choosing a part in the play was the easiest thing in the world. That's what bugged me about Peter – the boy had no angst. 'What about you, Emma?' he asked.

I stared at him furiously. 'You think I'm a pleb?' I demanded.

'No,' he said, raising his eyebrows in surprise. 'Not at all. I just wondered if . . . Well, I thought perhaps we could audition together.'

He was seriously deluded. Audition as a pleb? 'I don't think so,' I replied icily.

Peter shrugged his shoulders and turned back to the board but Kate tugged at my arm.

'Emma, don't you think Peter's on to something . . .' Then she stopped.

It's not often I lose it, but Kate's seen it once or twice. When the panic gets too much, I go into ultra-aggressive mode. It's a bit like a Quentin Tarantino film, only with more blood.

'Hmm, well, let's go and pick up the script and see what there is,' she said. The two of us linked arms and walked off in the direction of Mr Taylor's classroom. I thought I heard Peter scrabbling to keep up with us, but when I looked round he wasn't there.

Now, I'm not saying Mr Taylor's pathetic. But he is. He's one of those teachers who thinks he's still a student. He always needs a haircut and a shave and he hasn't got a clue how to dress. He wears those awful knitted ties, and jackets with elbow patches . . . and sandals. Plus there's the 'creative' side of Mr Taylor. He's a big fan of papier mâché and walking into his classroom is a bit like walking straight into someone else's bad dream, papier mâché grimacing angels and half-finished crocodiles hanging from the ceiling.

Kate and I knocked on the door of Mr Taylor's classroom and went in. There he was, making a papier mâché cactus. 'That looks nice, sir,' I piped up. Kate and I exchanged a meaningful glance.

'Ah, girls. What can I do for you?' He didn't bother looking up.

'We wanted copies of the script for *Samson and Delilah*, sir, thank you, sir,' said Kate.

He pointed over to a corner of the class-room and carried on dipping strips of news-paper in flour paste. Kate and I wandered over and picked up our copies of the script. As we then dashed to make our escape, he called out, 'Auditions tomorrow. Don't be late. Oh blast!' He'd managed to dunk his tie into the flour paste as he was leaning over to put a finishing touch to the cactus.

'One down, a million other foul ties to go,' I whispered. Kate and I snorted with laughter and ran out into the corridor. Once outside, we turned to the first page of the script and held our breath.

Samson and Delilah - the musical

Act One, Scene One

Exterior, market day. Lots of plebs calling out their wares from their stalls. Samson and his mother wandering through the market.

Plebians: Get your mongoose here!

Cacti! Two for the price of one!

Who will buy my luverly prunes?

Car stereos, ask no questions, half the price!

The crowd parts and Samson and his mother appear. Samson goes to pick something up from one of the stalls and immediately breaks it.

Samson: Oops, sorry, I don't know my own strength sometimes. (*Turning to his mother.*) Oh, Mother, do you think I'll ever meet a woman and fall in love?

Mother: Wash your mouth out, Samson!

Your life is devoted to God. Women are nothing but trouble. I should know, I'm one.

Samson: But does that mean I'll never wed? Do I have to spend my life alone?

Mother (*smugly*): You'll never be alone as long as you have God in your life, Samson.

Samson: I know. But it would be nice to have a little wife at home. Wouldn't it? (*Looking out pitifully into the audience.*)

The crowd forms into a choir behind Samson and he starts his song, Mother looking on disapprovingly:

I know that God's a good 'un
I guess he's on my side.
But I wish he'd care to give me
A cuddly Nazirite wife.

She doesn't have to be pretty
Or even all that nice
I just want someone around at
   home
Who isn't the dad of Christ.

Oh, where's the biblical wife of my
  dreams?
A Nazirite babe to take home?
My strength doesn't help in affairs
  of the heart
And I don't want to pray alone.

Kate and I looked at each other.

'Who wrote this?' I asked.

'What, with those papier mâché cacti? It has to be Taylor.'

'Nikky's not going to like Samson's ideas about a little wife.'

'You're telling me.'

We didn't know what else to say. We looked at the script; we looked back at each other. Then we burst out laughing.

'Oh, this is going to be entertaining, I'll say that much,' gasped Kate.

'Taylor's really done it this time,' I agreed, wheezing through the laughter. We were on the verge of full-blown hysteria, when the door to Mr Taylor's classroom was flung open.

'What's all the commotion?' he demanded testily. 'What's so funny? Emma, Kate, compose yourselves. I expect better of you two.'

He looked down at the scripts in our hands, then back at us as I wiped away a final tear. 'A lot of hard work has gone into that script. I'm expecting you both to take this project very seriously. I'll see you at the auditions tomorrow. Kate, make sure you start thinking about the character of Delilah. What are her motivations? Where is she coming from? That kind of thing.'

I waited for Mr Taylor to turn to me and give *me* some helpful direction, or even just to acknowledge me with more than a scowl. But he quickly retreated into his classroom, giving us a final shake of his head.

The two of us looked at the closed door for a second. Then Kate shoved me in the ribs before turning on her heel and running down the corridor. With a yelp I ran after her. As we walked out of the school gates, I tried hard not to think too much about the fact that Mr Taylor had almost completely failed to notice my existence.

CHAPTER FOUR

Kate did her best to help me. After all, she'd had a lifetime's experience of helping me. Helping me feel better, helping me not to feel left out, helping me to calm down. Ever felt like a charity case? Or a hopeless one? She came round to our house for tea and Mum made a real fuss of her, the same way everyone makes a fuss of Kate.

'Kate, darling! How are you, sweetie? You're looking prettier every day.'

'I'm very well, thank you, Mrs Hall. Mum says you were great as Titania last month.'

'Did she, darling? Did she really?' Mum asked, modestly pushing a curl of hair off her face. 'Oh, bless her. I mean, don't get me wrong. I *was* good, there's no denying that. But you know what it's like, darling. The small theatres . . . well, they just don't have the facilities, do they? But, darling, you! You'll be fantastic in this school musical.'

'Well, we don't know . . .'

'Oh, darling, we do. We do! Now, tell me all about it . . .'

It was a bit difficult to stomach. After all, Kate had come round to see me, not my mum and certainly not Titania. Eventually I got sick of watching the mutual fan club in action and dragged Kate to my bedroom.

'"Fairies, away!"' Mum called after us, waving regally from the bottom of the stairs. '"What, wilt thou hear some music, my sweet love?"' she continued as she wandered into the living room to the strains of Dad's new Beatles CD. We threw ourselves on to my bed and hid our faces in the quilt, trying to drown the sound of our laughter.

'Right, what part do you fancy playing?' Kate asked eventually, her face hot and red as she sat back up and flicked through the script. I straightened up too, suddenly sober.

Up until now I hadn't told Kate about my plans to try out as Delilah for one very good reason: I knew it was going to put us in the teensy bit awkward situation of going for the same part. Oh, Kate hadn't told me yet that she was going for Delilah, but I didn't need her to tell me. With a talent like hers, the whole school expected it. It would have been rude of her not to.

'What part are you going for?' I asked, stalling for time.

Kate looked up from the script, confused. 'Well, Delilah.' Then something passed across her face as she realized what I was thinking. 'You too?' she asked, with a smile of encouragement.

I took the script off her and pretended to read it, wondering if she felt sorry for me. I nodded, then looked back up at her questioningly. 'Well, why not?' I tried to laugh.

'Why not indeed?' she said brightly. I peered closely at her, but she didn't *seem* to be laughing at me. *Stop being so paranoid!* I told myself.

'Come on,' she said briskly. 'Let's find a good audition piece.' She looked up at me. 'I did promise to help you, didn't I?' Kate flicked through the script, finally jabbing a pen at one of the pages. 'Here we are! A good long scene for Delilah. This should be perfect.' I peered over Kate's shoulder and the two of us read through the scene:

Act Two, Scene Two
Interior, late at night.
Enter Delilah, stage left. She throws herself petulantly on to a couch.

Delilah's mum: What's wrong, sweetie-pie?
Delilah: What's wrong? What's wrong! I went out to the market today and not one person told me I was beautiful.
Delilah's mum: Darling, no!

Delilah stares spitefully at her mum.

Delilah: Haven't you forgotten something, Mother?

Delilah's mum rushes over with a plate of grapes, proffering them hopefully. Delilah looks away in disgust. The penny drops.

Delilah's mum: Forgive me, darling daughter. My breath was taken away by your ravishing beauty for a moment there. Yes, it's true: you are simply becoming more beautiful with each day that passes.

A pleb clearing the room in the background sniggers. Delilah leaps from the couch and turns on him.

Delilah: What are you sniggering at?

He cowers.

Pleb: Nothing, my lady.

Delilah narrows her eyes at him and then flounces away, looking out into the audience.

Delilah (*appealing to the audience*): Have you any idea how difficult it is being this beautiful? What, do you think this happens all on its own? Oh no, I'm up at the crack of dawn, down to the beauty parlour for arduous pampering, back home for a meagre breakfast of caviar and then the tire-

some chore of choosing yet another
toga to wear. It's exhausting and
that's before the day's even started
properly!

*Delilah outraged, Mum nodding sympa-
thetically in the background.*

I gulped. There were a lot of words to learn,
and that was just one part of one scene. *Plus*
there was the attitude. Delilah was a feisty girl.
I could do feisty in the safety of my own home
and surrounded by people who loved me and
laughed at my jokes. But up on stage?
The thought terrified me.

'Do you want to have a go,
Emma?' Kate offered me the
script. With a trembling
hand, I took it from her, the
spine already broken where
the pages had been bent
open.

I cleared my throat.
Kate nodded encouragingly.
I cleared my throat again.
Kate raised her eyebrows and leant forward,

waiting to hear me say my lines. 'I went . . . ?' she offered, prompting me.

I nodded my head firmly, resolved to get through at least *one* line of the script. I straightened my shoulders and began.

'I went to the market today . . .' I whispered, looking up at my friend, who was craning forward to hear me. I gulped. '. . . and not one, not one, erm, person said I was, well, you know . . .'

'Beautiful?' Kate finished the sentence for me. I nodded dumbly at her. Kate gently took the script back from me and tried not to look embarrassed. 'You don't believe what you're saying, do you?' she suggested, after a pause.

'What do you mean?' I asked, confused.

'Well, you're auditioning to play one of the most beautiful women in history.' I couldn't help a snort of laughter escaping. Kate raised a critical eyebrow at me. 'So you need to be convincing. You've got to sound as though you *believe* you're beautiful. Not as though you'd rather find a small rock to crawl under.'

'What about a middle-sized boulder?' I suggested hopefully, thinking Kate would laugh. She didn't even smile.

'You wanted me to help you,' she said. 'So I'm helping you. Now.' She shoved the script back into my hands. 'Once more. With feeling.'

I panicked. 'Gosh, is that the time?' I yelped, jumping off the bed. I pulled my friend up roughly and started propelling her towards the door. 'Wow, Kate, thanks. Thanks a lot. You've been a great help. But I really need you to go now, because, er, Mum will be calling me down for tea any minute. And I bet you need to get home anyway, don't you?'

Kate tried to protest as I jogged down the stairs, pulling her behind me. 'But, but . . . !'

'No buts, Kate! You've done more than enough already. That was great. Yeah, OK, bye, yeah, see you. Thanks a lot!'

The last thing I saw was Kate looking utterly confused. Then I shut the front door in my friend's face. With feeling.

As I turned to retreat up the stairs, Mum danced out of the lounge to the strains of 'Love Me Do'.

'Has Kate gone already? She should have stayed for tea,' Mum half-heartedly scolded as she waltzed into the kitchen.

'I did ask her, but she didn't want to,' I lied. I escaped up to my room and collapsed in a hot sweat on the bed. I looked at the script lying there accusingly and shoved it off on to the floor.

'You're not getting nervous about the play, are you, darling?' my mum trilled up the stairs as she heard the thump. I leapt off my bed and slammed my bedroom door shut in frustration. That's what I hate about mums. They know *everything*.

CHAPTER FIVE

When I burst through the doors of the assembly hall the next morning, I could barely believe my eyes. I was only ten minutes late, but already my fellow pupils seemed to have transformed themselves into extras from a pop video. There was Kathy Arnold, wearing – what were they? – leg warmers? She ran over to greet me and, yes, that really was a stupid sweatband round her head.

'Hi, Emma! Isn't this exciting?' I swear she'd adopted an American accent. I pushed past her and immediately tripped over Gareth . . . trying to do the splits.

'Gareth, what on earth do you think you're doing?' I asked the top of his head.

'Stretching exercises,' he grunted. 'I've put together a whole dance sequence that I thought

I could use in the production.'

'And who are you going to play, then?' I demanded.

'An ox,' he replied huffily, before crying out in pain as cramp took hold. I walked off, shaking my head in disbelief.

'Help me up!' he called after me.

I found my friends waiting outside Mr Taylor's classroom. They all looked almost as anxious as I felt, though it was difficult to tell *what* Nikky looked like behind the fake beard she was wearing. I knew from bitter experience that it wouldn't be a good idea to make a fuss at the sight of Nikky dressed up. She's the kind of girl who takes it as a personal insult if you tell her she looks nice. 'Cool beard, Nikky,' I said casually, gazing over in the opposite direction. She carelessly shrugged her shoulders as if to say, 'Oh, this old thing,' but I could tell she was pretty pleased with the effect.

'Yeah, well, you know.'

I managed to hide a smile.

I turned to Kate. Peter was sitting next to her, looking so laid back he was virtually sliding off the chair. 'Hi, Emma,' he said. I ignored him, still smarting from the suggestion that I was only fit to play a plebian.

'Erm, I said, "Hi, Emma"?' he tried again. Jeez, couldn't he take a hint?

'Emma, you're next on the —'

'Hi, Kate!' I interrupted, shoving him out of the way to give my *real* friend a big hug.

'Oh, you're speaking to me now, then?' Kate asked. 'What was all that about last night, pushing me out of the door like that?' I'd been hoping Kate would have conveniently decided not to be offended by my behaviour the night before. I wasn't sure I could cope with explaining myself. Not when I was so nervous about auditions.

'I'm sorry,' I said, my phoney smile wavering. Kate stared at me hard, as though she wanted to say much more, then she shook her head with a sigh and obviously decided to let it go.

'Emma, Peter is trying to tell you that you're next on the list of people to audition. Where've you been? We've not had a chance to run through our piece!'

I gulped. Where had I been? I'd been looking for my lucky socks, that's where I'd been.

(I'm not kidding. I was in such a state I was clinging on to anything that might help.) But my lucky socks had been in the wash. That was Mum again – ruining my life as per usual.

'Next!' screeched Mr Taylor. I looked at my friends and almost felt like crying, they looked so sorry for me. But there was nothing else for it. Silently, I walked into the classroom as Kathy Taylor brushed past doing a *pas de deux*.

It took a while for my eyes to adjust. The curtains were shut against the morning sun and a single bare bulb lit up the room, hanging directly over Mr Taylor's head. He'd really gone to town on the wardrobe front, and even I had to admit he looked the part. A cheap, imitation-silk cravat adorned his throat and he was wearing a slightly grubby satin jacket. It was kind of Oscar Wilde meets John Travolta. He pointed to the centre of the room and said nothing.

I bustled over, managing to drop my script in my haste. I bent over to pick it up, hoping to stumble across my lost dignity somewhere on the way.

'And you are?' Taylor drawled.

'Erm,' I hesitated. Would he really take me seriously as Delilah? I decided to stall for time. 'I'm Emma, sir.'

'Yes, yes, yes!' he hissed. 'We all know that, don't we? What *character* are you playing?'

'Delilah, sir?' As I gripped my hands together to stop them from trembling, I watched Taylor scratch a large cross on to the form he was holding. He jerked his head back up and glared at me.

'Go on, then,' he commanded. What had happened to this man? He'd gone from being a big wimp to the sadist of the staffroom. (And that was saying something.) He folded his arms and waited.

This was it, then. My big moment. This was my chance to prove I had what it took to set the world alight – or at least the school stage. I cleared my throat and tried to remember what Kate had told me. I needed to *believe* I was beautiful. I also needed to know my lines, so it was a shame I'd stubbornly ignored the copy of the script that Kate had left with me the night before.

'And from the top,' Mr Taylor prompted, leaning back in his chair.

I opened my mouth to speak but no sound came out. I was feeling light-headed and nauseous. Perhaps I would faint and be given the lead role out of sympathy? Mr Taylor was staring hard at me now and I realized I couldn't just stand there forever. I had to do *something*.

'Everything OK, Emma?' our teacher asked, staring quizzically. I nodded dumbly. Mr Taylor raised a critical eyebrow towards Mrs Rogers, sitting at the piano. He turned his head to one side and whispered out of the side of his mouth, 'This is going to take a miracle.' Mrs Rogers adjusted her bust in silent, but damning agreement.

'Ha! Ha! Ha! Ha!' I laughed out loud, inwardly horrified at the level of noise I seemed to be making. Had I completely lost control of my body?

'I beg your pardon?' Mr Taylor asked, looking quickly over each shoulder to see if something had happened behind his back.

'I heard what you said,' I told him, trying to pretend that I enjoyed the sarcastic joke he'd made at my expense. Mr Taylor ducked his head behind his clipboard to hide the expression on his face.

'Oh, don't worry, I'm not offended,' I continued. 'I'm sure it must be very difficult for you, dealing with a stellar talent like mine.' I think I was having what they call a 'flash of clarity'. I didn't hear any thunderbolt but at that moment I suddenly saw that this whole audition had been out of the window before I'd even stepped into the room. It was kind of liberating. Realizing what a loser you are can have its benefits. I didn't care what Mr Taylor thought of me now.

'Ah,' he said hesitantly. 'Well, Emma. One never knows, does one? You may indeed have an extraordinary talent. That's why we're here. To find it . . .' His voice trailed off, as he failed to convince even himself that he was about to discover my brilliant Oscar-winning talent as an actress. I don't know if it was just the guilt kicking in, but it seemed he was willing to give me another chance.

He spread a hand out in front of him and raised his eyebrows, indicating that my second chance was happening now. 'So. Delilah. From the top!'

'I went to the market today . . .' I began hesitantly.

The classroom door thumped open, ricocheting off the wall and giving me my second nervous breakdown of the morning. It was Mr Inglethorp, our school caretaker.

'Don't mind me! Just pretend I'm not here,' he stage-whispered, before doing pantomime tiptoes along the outside edge of the classroom. I was mortified. This is just what I *didn't* need – an audience. I'd been given a second chance and now even other people besides myself were helping to blow it.

Mr Inglethorp was pointing exaggeratedly towards his broom that was resting against the far wall, just so that we were all completely clear on why he was here, ruining my audition.

I gulped and forced myself to continue. '. . . to the market today and not a single person . . .'

'Ooh, she's good, isn't she?' I heard Mr Inglethorp say enthusiastically as he passed Mrs Rogers at the piano. Mrs Rogers let out an audible guffaw of what could only be described as incredulous disbelief.

'. . . said I was beautiful,' I finished flatly, my voice as tiny as I felt.

'Said she's what?' Mr Inglethorp asked loudly. 'What was that?'

'Beautiful,' snapped Mrs Rogers, shaking her head.

'Oh aye, she is that,' he agreed enthusiastically, leaning on the broom handle, clearly in no rush to depart the scene of groundbreaking theatre. 'Well, it's her mother, isn't it? Got those actress good looks to hand down to her, hasn't she?'

I stared at Mr Taylor, my face burning, trying hard to pretend our caretaker wasn't there. Mr Taylor stared back at me. 'That will be all, Emma,' he said finally, scribbling something beside my name. 'I'm very impressed by your . . . erm . . . talents. And ambition. I'm sure there's a place in the play for you . . . I think . . .' He was starting to look embarrassed. 'Ahem, well, that's enough for now.' The man couldn't even meet my eye any more. 'If you can just send the next person in. Thanks a lot. I mean that.'

'Well done, Emma!' called out Mr Inglethorp as I slipped out of the classroom.

'She's very good, isn't she?' was the last thing I heard him say.

When I emerged into the assembly hall, my hands were still shaking. My friends crowded round and Nikky pulled aside her beard and demanded, 'How was it?' Everyone looked at me anxiously. They hadn't had their auditions yet and it was up to me to make them feel OK.

I burst into tears.

Peter immediately put his arm round me and pulled out a crumpled tissue for me to blow my nose into. I was too preoccupied with bawling my eyes out to shrug him off, so I took the tissue and hooted into it.

I was steered towards a chair, and Nikky, Kate and Peter knelt at my feet making reassuring noises until Nikky's patience ran out. 'Oh, for God's sake, you big girl's blouse, you're letting the sisterhood down. It can't have been that bad!'

I peered at my friends from behind Peter's disintegrating tissue. 'No, it wasn't that bad.' For a moment my poor friends looked hopeful.

'It was worse.' Their faces fell. Even Nikky

didn't know what to say for once. Peter squeezed my hand, but this time I pushed him away. 'I was terrible, truly terrible,' I said woefully. They all loyally shook their heads and hushed 'no's' at me.

'I was,' I assured them. 'I couldn't even cope when Mr Inglethorp barged his way in. How would I cope in front of an entire audience?' Just then Mr Taylor poked his head round the classroom door. 'Kate, I think we're ready for you now. I'm really looking forward to this!'

Kate had the decency to look embarrassed and quickly followed Mr Taylor into his class-room. 'Good luck!' whispered Peter and Nikky. Kate looked round and smiled grimly at them. She tried to catch my eye, but I glanced away. I looked up again just in time to see the door shut behind her.

'Don't worry,' Peter reassured me. 'Kate's sure to do OK.' I shoved his snotty tissue back at him and walked off.

☆ ☆ ☆

I didn't hang about that morning to find out how Kate did, but I didn't need to. In first break the whisper radiated around the playground like a fresh piece of celebrity gossip straight out of *Hot!* magazine. As I sat on the school steps, I could see the news physically spreading. Kerry Doyle dragged Phil Bramley to one corner of the playground and whispered excitedly into his ear. Phil looked pretty excited himself. Then he went off to play a game of football with the lads, but not until he'd pulled John Reeves to one side and muttered something beneath his breath, with John shaking his head in disbelief. John tracked down his sister, Pippa, in the year below and told her everything, and she'd pulled out her mobile and sent a group text message. Which is when my phone jumped about in my blazer pocket and I knew I couldn't put off the inevitable any longer. With a sense of dread, I pulled my phone out and clicked on the button to see who the text was from. Pippa. I opened up the text message and felt the butterflies in my stomach turn to worms as I read:

Kate 2 B Delilah. Taylor recommending stage school.

'Of course she is. And of course he is,' I said grimly.

'You keep talking to yourself like that, people are going to start worrying.' It was Nikky. 'That's the second time this week I've caught you doing that,' she added.

A boy twice our size, from the year above, tried to walk past us towards the woodwork block and without even looking around Nikky casually stepped out into his path. She stopped talking to me and looked up at him, raising her eyebrows and holding a hand out. She had all the cool aplomb and icy authority of a mafia mobster. The boy bristled, putting his shoulders back. After all, he did tower above my skinny friend. She cocked her head on one side as a warning. The only warning he would get. The boy was so shocked at Nikky's nerve, he barely knew what he was doing as he dug into his school bag, pulled out his packed lunch and handed it over.

'Good man,' Nikky told him jovially as she settled down beside me and nodded him on his way. I watched him leave.

I put my head in my hands. 'God, Nikky. The humiliation,' I groaned, referring to my performance that morning.

'I know,' she agreed. 'It's great, isn't it?'

I looked at her in horror. This was not the level of sympathy I had been hoping for.

'Ah. I take it you're not talking about that boy,' she said, offering me one of his Eccles cakes. I shook my head. 'How *did* she do, anyway?'

'Kate?' Nikky asked.

I nodded glumly.

'As it happens, absolutely brilliantly. Which we all knew anyway. So I don't know why you're getting so upset about it.' Nikky pulled her God beard out of her backpack and gazed at it fondly. She moved a hand to stroke it, but then seemed to remember that I was there and hurriedly stuffed the fake wool beard back into her bag. 'Emma. You can't go trying to judge yourself against people who are just completely different to you.'

'I'm not!' I argued, my voice high and tight with outrage.

'You're not arguing with me, are you?' Nikky asked, swivelling round on the step to look me in the face.

'No, no,' I said, quickly remembering who I was talking to.

'Good.' She let out a sigh. 'Look, Emma. If I tried to be like most of the girls in this school, I'd be miserable too. You and Kate are such good friends, but she has this golden layer to her life and the rest of us do not. We never will have. So don't send yourself mad trying to be like her – just enjoy being her best friend.'

Nikky's speech was too much after all the day's emotions, and a lump was definitely forming in my throat. I wondered if Nikky would forgive me this once for getting emotional. But my sentimental moment was interrupted by a loud yelp, and when I looked up there was an empty space where Nikky had been sitting. I looked to either side of me – nothing.

'Up here!' came a strangulated cry. I looked above my head and saw Nikky restrained by our headmaster's fat grip. He was holding her at arm's length as she kicked and struggled to break free. Suddenly he loosened his grip and Nikky fell in a pile of flailing limbs. Still hissing and bristling, she leapt to her feet, her fists swirling in preparation for the first punch.

'Young lady, don't even think about it,' warned Mr Key.

'Don't you call me "young lady"!' Nikky protested indignantly.

'I've had just about enough of your antics, *young lady*. You do not steal other people's school lunches,' said Mr Key, ignoring Nikky's protests. 'However big they may be.' A hesitant face peered round from behind Mr Key. It was the towering Eccles Cake Boy.

Nikky glowered, then looked round at me. 'Save yourself while you can,' she said, indicating with a jerk of her thumb that I should make myself scarce.

'One more word from you and you can kiss God goodbye,' warned Mr Key, looking significantly at the fake beard that still poked out of Nikky's bag. That was the ultimate threat and Nikky reluctantly gave in and followed our headmaster back to his office, still huffing and puffing all the way.

'She's going to have to learn,' said a familiar voice from behind me. I looked round and saw Peter shaking his head in amusement.

'Actually, she was trying to be nice to me,' I said.

'Probably was,' he agreed. We smiled grimly at each other as the end-of-break bell rang out. 'You heard about –?' Peter started to say.

'Yeah, I heard,' I interrupted, before I had to listen to the painful details all over again. Peter gave me a sympathetic poke in the arm. Then Kate came running up, her face flushed with excitement.

'Emma! Emma! Did you hear?'

I told her I'd heard and gave her a hug. It turned out Kate had been in the school staffroom all break while Mr Taylor and Mrs Rogers tried to talk to her about the different stage schools she could apply for.

'I mean, in their dreams. I've got better things to do than that. Like I want to be around those spoilt prima donna kids? Or anyone else when I've got you? Right, Emma?'

'Right,' I agreed, hoping I sounded more convincing than I felt. We walked back towards the school building, Kate linking her arm through mine and Peter following behind. As I pulled the door open and stepped back to allow both of them to walk past me into the school corridor, Peter hung back a bit. He gave me a fat wink, then he whispered, 'We'll make an actress of you yet.'

'Has my ickle, wickle Sammy-wammy been a good boy? Has he? Yes? He's a good boy, isn't he?' These were the words that greeted me when I got home. Dad was hanging over the bars of Sam's playpen, tickling him all over and talking to my brother like he was the idiot son of the family. I don't mind Sam being spoilt; he is quite cute after all. But I do mind having to listen to my dad talking in babyspeak – he's old enough to know better.

'Shouldn't you be out supporting your family?' I asked.

'Stocktake. Don't need me. Isn't that right, Sammy-wammy?' he replied, barely lifting his head out of the playpen.

I left them to it and went to find my mum in the kitchen. She was up to her elbows in soap-suds, washing the pots and plates so that she could start making tea. A copy of *The Stage* lay open on the kitchen table. I picked up a tea towel and started drying. Mum looked at me, worried.

'Everything OK?' she asked eventually.

'Yep,' I replied.

'Only, I'm not used to seeing you with a tea towel in your hand. Are you feeling all right? No nasty bump to the head or anything?'

Oh yes, very funny, ha, ha, Mother.

'No, things are not all right,' I told her. 'The audition was a complete disaster.' I had to look away because the expression on Mum's face was not good. I was disappointed myself, without having to see her look as though the end of the world had arrived.

'Oh, darling. All actors and actresses hate auditions. And we all have a terrible audition story. I remember the time when . . .'

'Not now, Mum,' I interrupted as I sank into a chair. She managed to look guilty, though she could just have been acting. You never know with my mum.

'So what happened then?' she changed tack. 'Did the scenery fall down? Were you projecting your voice enough? You know what I've told you about that.' She paused and looked sympathetic. 'Was the director a pig?' she demanded.

'None of those things. No. It was all my fault. I couldn't get a sentence out of my mouth. I was hopeless.' And I burst into tears.

With his usual perfect timing, Dad popped his head round the door. 'Everything all right in here?' he asked, forcing a jolly tone into his voice. Mum had swept me up in a big hug so my face was stuck to her chest and I couldn't see a thing, but from the swish of her bosom I could tell she was signalling something over the top of my head.

'What's that?' Dad asked. 'What are you trying to say, Mary?' I felt more frantic signalling going on. Then Dad coughed in an embarrassed, man-type way and I heard him shut the door as he retreated from the kitchen, back to Sam.

'Do you want to talk about it?' Mum asked. I wrenched myself out of her iron grip and shook my head. Mum peered into my face.

'Are you sure?' Hesitantly, I changed the shake into a slow nod. I focused on the floor for a few moments as Mum lowered herself into the chair next to mine, pushing the last dirty plates out of the way. She waited.

'I just don't know what's wrong with me,' I started, not sure if this was going to make me feel any better. 'You're *brilliant* at showing off. Why can't I be?' I asked Mum, who was busy trying not to look offended by what I'd just said. 'I mean, no offence, like,' I added quickly as an afterthought. 'Why can't I be more . . . well, less . . . well . . .' I couldn't finish the sentence. It would have killed me to say 'more like you' to my mum of all people.

Mum sat back and folded her arms. 'Oh, darling. Do you know, when I was your age I was exactly the same.' I looked up at her in surprise and she gave me a slow and meaning-ful nod. 'Do you know what it took to get *me* on stage for my first school play? Nana physically shoving me on from the wings!'

Mum screeched with laughter at the memory, making me wince.

'And do you know why? Because I was convinced that everyone else was so much better than me. That I would be the only person fluffing my lines.' Mum shook her beaded necklace angrily. 'But do you know what the joke is? That night, almost everyone messed up. We were all as nervous as each other. You see, everyone else feels *exactly* the same way as you. We all go through life thinking all the other people know what they're doing. And you know what? None of us do. Not even –' she paused dramatically – '*the grown-ups.*'

I looked at her cynically. 'It's true,' she said firmly. 'I wasn't born with a natural ability to show off, you know. I had to work long and hard at it.' Mum grinned at me.

'I know I can annoy you, Emma. I don't mean to. But I was like you once, believe me. The thing is, once I'd found my confidence, I didn't ever want to let go of it again. That's why I am like I am – even if it is embarrassing sometimes. I know you and your dad are angels for putting up with me, and I do appreciate it.' She stood up and shook herself dramatically as if chasing the sombre mood away. 'Now. How about an ice cream?'

CHAPTER SIX

I was feeling much better the next morning. I might not have got the part of Delilah, but after my chat with Mum, some of my confidence had been restored. OK, so I might not be the lead, but Best Supporting Actress sounded pretty good too. I still saw a glimmer of hope.

As I set out for school Mum ran up to give me a dramatic hug. 'Don't forget, darling,' she called down the street, waving Sam's pudgy hand at me in a mock goodbye. 'You can't go wrong with me as your mother!' I shook my head as she shut the front door on the sound of her own laughter.

I waited for Kate as usual by the park, but yet again she didn't turn up. It wasn't just that I felt foolish hanging around on my own with only Mrs Brown and her stupid Labrador for company. It hurt my feelings. A lot. You know how a toddler looks when the ice cream falls off the top of his cornet into the grass and dirt? Everyone around laughs and chucks him under the chin, but let me tell you, that kid is devastated. Well, I didn't feel that bad – let's not overplay things here. But heck, bad enough. Kate hadn't knocked the ice cream off my cornet, but she'd definitely taken a bite out of my ninety-nine flake. And it didn't make me feel any better when she sent another text message, with another perfectly reasonable explanation as to why she'd abandoned me.

Stayed at Dad's last night. See you at school. Soz.

I set off for school on my lonesome again and stepped into the assembly hall to be greeted by one totally weird scene:

'The carpenter's hammer goes tap, tap, tap
and his saw goes see, saw, see
and he planes and he measures

and he hammers and he saws
while he builds his house for me.'

Mr Inglethorp was putting the final
touches to the school stage. He was
wearing a carpenter's belt with little pockets
for nails and spirit levels and other tools I didn't
know the names of. He had a stubby pencil
shoved behind his ear and, yes, that really was
a song he was strangling. Didn't he know that
caretakers didn't sing?

Mr Inglethorp looked up and greeted me
with a cheery, 'Eh up, chuck. That's right, come
along, get to your class. Don't mind me.' I
sidled past him with my head down.

'Brilliant,' he remarked to himself with a
slow, awed shake of his head, interrupting his
work to watch me walk past. 'Ruddy brilliant
you were in that audition yesterday.'

'Not good enough for Delilah, though, was I?'
I muttered, sulkily kicking a corner of the stage.

'Eh, watch that!' Mr Inglethorp warned.
'Took me half the night, that did. Anyway,
don't you worry yourself about the play. What
will be will be.'

He indicated with a nod of his head that I should look over my shoulder, and then he bent down to pat the corner of the stage, as if consoling it. I turned round just in time to see Kate wander into the assembly hall.

'Kate?'

I swear she jumped a foot into the air.

'What? Oh, hi.' She flushed and looked guilty. I noticed another figure stroll into the assembly hall behind Kate and as he wandered past, hastily snatching a glance at my friend, I recognized Edward Ponsford. Edward is what you might call a 'school character'. He hangs around the park with his mates, knows how to shuffle cards like a croupier, and can do wheelies on his mountain bike. Suddenly from behind my back I heard Edward yelping as his form teacher grabbed his ear and dragged him into a classroom. Kate heard the commotion and looked over my shoulder in time to see Edward's feet disappearing through the classroom door. But when Kate shifted her glance back to me, she wasn't laughing . . . she looked concerned. Like she *cared* what happened to Edward Ponsford.

It didn't take long for my razor-sharp brain to put two and two together and make . . . well, whatever it is you make. A half-forgotten memory of those two sunlit, anonymous figures in the park suddenly snapped back into my brain and I realized that there was a very good reason why Kate hadn't been walking to school with me in the mornings.

'What's going on?' I asked.

'Nothing,' Kate answered, carefully lowering her eyes to the floor, which only confirmed my suspicions. I wouldn't have called what I was feeling *jealousy* exactly. But I was. Feeling jealous, I mean.

'What was it you said yesterday?' I asked hotly. '"Why do I need anyone else when I've got you?" Weren't those the words?' I still hadn't even mentioned Edward, but we both knew who and what we were talking about. Betrayal.

I could understand Kate having other friends, but this was more than that. It was *a boy*. And I could even just about understand one of those. After all, we managed to tolerate

Peter well enough, but Peter had been around forever. This was different. If a girl our age suddenly starts hanging around with a boy, out of the blue like that, it means something. I'd seen it already, the way that certain characters at school had started to take an interest in each other. Next thing you knew, they were calling themselves boyfriend and girlfriend and hanging around in corners of the playground, ignoring everyone else. It was downright unsettling. All the way through school, we'd all known the rules and stuck to them rigidly. Now suddenly things were changing. And if Kate was starting to hang out with a boy, that was double worrying. Because next time I had a knicker-twisting session, how did I know my friend was going to be there for me? After all, she hadn't been for the past two mornings. Panic flooded me. Kate still hadn't said anything and I guess I should have shut up, but I was like a runaway train. I blew.

'I assume *he*'s the reason you've left me standing on my own like a lemon for the past two mornings?'

SWALK

Kate started walking away from me, but I stalked after her. After all, it's hard to stay calm when you're talking to someone's shoulder blades. And let's face it, I wasn't trying very hard. Kate slowed down to a halt and turned round to face me.

'*Thank* you,' I said, struggling to keep a reasonable tone in my voice.

'I'm sorry,' Kate began, looking anywhere rather than at me.

'You're not making me feel any better,' I said.

Kate shrugged her shoulders helplessly. 'OK, so I've started being friends with Edward. That's no big deal, is it?' she asked, jostling me and trying to slip her hand into mine. But I couldn't say anything back. *If it wasn't such a big deal,* I thought, *why didn't you mention it in the first place?* Eventually, after about 60 million years, I found the strength to shrug my shoulders.

'No big deal,' I forced myself to agree, finally giving my friend's hand a squeeze. The sudden dangerous reality of falling out with Kate on top of all my other reasons for near-nervous collapse was too much. But there was no way I believed what I was saying. Thank the Sweet

Lord Almighty, Miss Cameron swooped into the assembly hall. 'Into the classroom, girls, quick sharp. We're late for register and this will never do.' She grabbed hold of Kate's hand and dragged her away. I followed the two of them into our classroom.

Once we were inside, Miss Cameron began her ritual plea for quiet. 'Girls and boys, quieten down now, please. Shush now. Please. Could you possibly keep it down, I want to take the register. SHUUUT UPPP!'

Everyone shut their gobs fast. No one particularly wanted their eardrums blasted. Miss Cameron is a sweetie, but you don't want to mess with her in the mornings. We'd all learnt that the hard way.

She put her mug of strong black coffee down on her desk, stifled a yawn and started reading out everyone's names. And this morning even Dave Pilchard didn't try playing up. Then Miss Cameron pulled a list out from among her pile of books. Tucking a stray wisp of hair behind her ear, she raised her head and squinted at us from behind her glasses.

'Before we get on with lessons, I need to make an announcement. Several of you took part in the auditions yesterday. Well done to all of you for showing willing. After a long and difficult selection process, Mr Taylor has chosen the cast for *Samson and Delilah*.' She paused. The tension was awful. I shoved my hands under my legs to cool them against the wood of the chair. I looked across at Kate, but she was hiding behind the pages of an exercise book. Here it was. The Big Announcement. I just had to sit tight and get through the next few minutes. I know it seems incredible now, but there was a tiny, optimistic part of my brain that still hoped there might have been a last-minute change of mind and I might have wangled the part of Delilah. It was like waiting to see who was Number One in the Top Forty on a Sunday evening. Except worse. I saw Peter smiling at me encouragingly from the other side of the classroom. It made me feel better, but I wouldn't admit that to Peter by smiling back.

'I'm going to let you know which members of the class will be taking part in the play. Dave Pilchard, you're going to be an innkeeper.

Nikky, Mr Taylor was very impressed with your effort. Despite certain unfortunate events since your audition, he and Mr Key had to think long and hard . . . but they have decided that you can play God. Needless to say, however, we expect immaculate behaviour for the rest of term.'

Nikky punched her fist into the air and whooped.

'Peter, well done, you're a pleb. Johnny, you'll be . . .'

My eyes were fixed on our teacher, but I hardly heard anything she was saying any more. I was just waiting for her to get to my name. The classroom had reduced to a pinpoint of concentration and I scowled at Nikky as she cheerily started to whistle to herself through her teeth. She stopped whistling sharply and bared her teeth to growl at me.

Then Miss Cameron said my name. This was it. This was the moment of truth.

'Emma, Mr Taylor has decided that he needs you to play . . . Third Donkey.'

At exactly the same time that my world fell apart, the entire class burst out laughing. 'Ha, Emma's a right old donkey! I always knew that!' exclaimed Dave Pilchard. Thank you, David.

Miss Cameron hurried on, looking embarrassed on my behalf.

'And finally, I'm very pleased to announce that, Kate, you'll be playing Delilah.'

The classroom erupted into spontaneous cheers and applause.

I couldn't believe it. This was much worse than I could ever have thought possible. It wasn't just that I'd been rejected as Delilah. It wasn't just that it confirmed that Kate had been given the main part. Mr Taylor thought I had the acting skills of a donkey.

CHAPTER SEVEN

We'd heard rumours about who would be playing Samson, but Mr Taylor was reluctant to confirm the casting. 'I'm still auditioning,' he'd say impatiently as we trailed after him out of the school door to his car. 'There are a number of options.'

'Is Peter one?' Nikky asked cheekily, pointing at Peter and laughing behind her hand. Peter smiled along with her, unruffled by her gentle teasing.

Even Mr Taylor couldn't help grinning. 'Possibly, possibly . . .' he'd say mysteriously, before slamming the door to his clapped-out rust bucket shut and attempting to start it up. We got bored after listening to the engine cough and choke for a third time and wandered off to sit on the school steps.

Obviously, Samson would have to be tall, strong and good-looking. None of us could think of a single boy in our year who answered that description.

'There's always Steve Gunneridge,' Peter suggested. We all paused to consider the snotty nose and collapsing socks that made Steve Gunneridge born to be a hero.

'Or Phil Branson?' interrupted Nikky, wiping the back of her hand across her nose. Of course she'd nominate him. He was second only to her in his thuggery.

'What about Mark Jessop?' I ventured, before remembering that the most astounding thing about Mark Jessop was his ability to fall asleep in the middle of class.

'Oh well, we'll find out on Monday,' Peter commented philosophically as Mr Inglethorp eventually bustled us off the steps and out of the school gates.

☆ ☆ ☆

'What's your mum making tonight?' Peter asked as we parted company at the corner of Church Lane.

'I don't even want to think about it,' I

answered, grimacing and kicking the trunk of the conker tree.

The two of us stood for a moment in companionable silence. A conker fell to the ground between us and Peter bent down to pick it up, holding it out to me. I shook my head. 'You have it,' I said. 'I need to be getting back before Mum calls the police.' I started to walk backwards away from him. '*Hopefully* I'll still be alive for rehearsals next week.'

Peter laughed and called after me, 'Remember. If you can't identify what it is or where it came from, don't eat it.' Then he walked off, waving a hand casually over his shoulder at me.

On Monday morning, as we arranged ourselves on the cold tiles of the assembly hall's floor, Kate leant over to whisper in my ear. 'I know who's going to be Samson,' she said, tugging at one of her blonde plaits in excitement. One of the few faults Kate has is she's terrible at keeping a secret to herself. I glanced at Peter and Nikky, who were too busy going through their lines to hear our conversation.

'Well, why didn't you say so on Friday?' I asked, shifting my backpack round behind me to lean on.

'I couldn't! I only found out last night,' Kate whispered gleefully. 'Edward came round to my house and told me.' I felt a muscle in my eyelid twitch.

'What? He told you who's going to be Samson? But how would he know that?' I asked.

'Look. No time now, Mr Taylor's here,' she said, nodding towards the stage.

'So who *is* playing Samson?' I hissed.

She shook her head helplessly. 'You'll see,' was all she said.

I turned round just in time to see Mr Taylor walk past. Kids gathered nervously in huddles as he marched up the assembly hall. He'd given all of us a pretty rough time during auditions and we weren't sure whether or not he'd returned to his usual, incompetent self yet. As soon as he tripped over the corner of the stage, we knew we were safe. He cleared his throat and fiddled with his tie. (Orange tweed and looked like it had shrunk in the wash.)

'Welcome, everyone, to the first day of rehearsals. I hope you've all been learning your lines, because we don't have much time before the Big Day. I'm counting on each and every one of you to do your best. Now, I want the choir to come and sit in front of the stage here. That's right. OK, this morning we're going to run through the opening scene. So, to begin with, Samson could you please make your way to the stage?'

Nikky and Peter gripped each other's hands, Peter blindly reaching out for mine as his eyes stayed glued to the stage. I let his fingers wrap round mine and watched all my friends hold their breath. Even Kate was holding her breath, and she *knew* who Samson was. I squeezed Peter's hand and he turned his head towards me just for a minute to wink. I sighed impatiently. This was all a laugh for him.

We turned back to the stage, our eyes searching the crowd of uniforms to see if there was any movement. Suddenly we could see someone jostling through. It was, it was . . .

'Oh my God,' whispered Kate. Her eyes widened in delight, enjoying the drama of the moment. As I saw a figure push his way through the scrum of kids I felt my hand slowly loosen its grip on Peter's, and then fall by my side.

Edward Ponsford strolled towards the centre of the stage and stood with one hip jutting out – just like the models in my mum's catalogue. The script dangled carelessly from a hand and he shoved the other into the pocket of his jeans. Jeans! Everyone knew what Mr Key thought about the wearing of jeans. You had to hand it to Edward. He knew how to live life on the edge.

Mr Taylor joined him on the stage. 'Ahem, Sarah is off sick today so I'll be stepping in as Samson's mother.' He glared round the hall, daring anyone to laugh. Nikky clamped her hands over her mouth, but a snigger still escaped. Fortunately, Mr Taylor had already turned his attention to the script.

'OK, Edward. Let's take it from the top.' Wearily, Edward lifted his script and roughly pushed a hand through his hair. Even I had to admit he had charisma. As if that wasn't enough, as Edward began reading from the script – 'Oh, Mother, do you think I'll ever meet a woman and fall in love?' – I swear I heard a hundred female knees knocking together.

My gaze turned back to Kate and I watched her as she sat looking dreamily at Edward. That was when I knew without a shadow of a doubt, that there was no way I could ever compete. Given the choice between Loyal Best Friend and Charismatic New Boyfriend . . . well, there was no choice. Charismatic New Boyfriend was going to win every time.

As the bell for first break rang out, we all reluctantly turned away from the stage and wandered out towards the playground. 'My, my, my *Delilah*!' sang one of Edward's friends as he danced past us, swirling his hips like an ancient crooner and pointing gleefully at Kate. I couldn't help scowling at him.

'What's your problem?' he asked, before

departing with a final twirl of his hips. Kate was laughing, *encouraging* him.

'He seems to think Edward's your boyfriend,' I told her. But she'd already switched her mobile on and now it rang out with text message alerts. She bent her head to read them and held the phone close to her face.

'Did you hear what I said?' I asked the top of her head.

'Mmmm,' she mumbled, before bursting out laughing and putting her phone away. I raised my eyebrows at her, but she pretended not to notice, refusing to share the joke with me as she walked towards the school doors and out into the playground.

I watched my friend's retreating back in astonishment. We *always* read each other's text messages. I ran after her. 'So, is he your boyfriend?' I asked again, more forcefully this time. I still couldn't bring myself to use his name.

Kate sighed. 'If you mean Edward, then no, Emma, he's not my boyfriend.' She raised her eyes heavenwards to indicate that the whole subject was boring her.

'Sorry to be such a pain,' I said sarcastically.

Kate shook her head and pushed past me, trying to avoid a confrontation. I ran after her and grabbed her by the shoulder. She turned round. 'Look, Emma, it's . . .'

'Yeah, I know. It's No Big Deal,' I interrupted angrily. 'So if it's no big deal, why didn't you ever tell me about him? Why are you hiding your text messages from me?'

She looked at her shoes, gleaming next to my scuffed ones. 'He's not my boyfriend,' she said again, this time in a very small voice.

'Not yet, he isn't,' I answered, and walked off.

☆ ☆ ☆

Do you want to know what hell is? Hell is getting through a school day when you've fallen out with your best friend. It was all well and good walking away from Kate in the school playground, but how was I supposed to maintain that level of hostility when everything about school forced us together? There's not a teacher in the world who will announce, 'And today, girls and boys, we're all going to swap places because Emma is freezing out her best friend, Kate. Chop! Chop! There's a moody silence to be upheld here.' It ain't gonna happen. And even if I had been able to get away from Kate, there still wouldn't be anyone else to sit next to. Because everyone has their own best friend who they sit next to in class. Even Nikky and Peter seem to have some invisible school superglue keeping them sitting in the same pair of desks, despite the fact that Peter can't play football and everyone knows Nikky hates boys who can't play football.

'Can I squeeze in with you two?' I asked sheepishly as we wandered back into class.

'Don't be stupid,' Nikky replied, looking at me, horrified.

'You know you can't,' said Peter reasonably.

With a sense of doom I walked towards the desk I shared with Kate. She was already there, looking rigidly to the front of the room, her chin high and her mouth pursed. She didn't even flinch at the high-pitched screech that came from the metal frame of the chair when I scraped it back to sit down.

During the lesson I didn't bother listening to Miss Cameron's enthusiastic talk about Victorians . . . or Edwardians . . . or whoever it was. I was too busy concentrating on the textbook that Kate and I were sharing. It was bent and broken from years of scholarly abuse, but that wasn't the point. The point was that a tiny, but fierce battle was taking place across our desks. Kate held the left-hand page open and I had my hand over the corner of the right-hand page. Both of our fingertips were white with exertion, as we pulled from right to left, fighting to achieve domination of the book. It was cheap and petty, but I think it probably made both of us feel better. As Miss Cameron rambled on about poor ickle child chimney sweeps, she had no idea what kind of a deadly serious game was being played out in the far left-hand corner of the classroom under the harvest-festival frieze.

As soon as lunchtime arrived we both kicked back our chairs in disgust and gave each other truly foul looks. It was out in the open now. I felt sick with misery and it was a cruel and hollow victory when Kate slid her eyes away first. It didn't make me feel good at all. Frankly, I wanted to burst into tears.

Kate pushed past me towards the school canteen and Nikky and Peter stood by the classroom door, watching Kate's retreating back. 'What's happened?' Peter asked, as I reached him and Nikky. The two of them looked puzzled and unhappy. That's the problem with falling out with your best friend. It's called the Ripple Effect. (I think some scientist somewhere has probably written a thesis on this, possibly inspired by falling out with his own best friend.) The Ripple Effect means that it's not just you and your best friend who get to feel miserable when you fall out. Your other friends do too.

'We've fallen out,' I explained guiltily.

'Oh, great,' sighed Nikky, wasting no time in letting me know how pleased she was with this turn of events. 'I guess that means we're all going to have a miserable lunchtime now. Well, count me out.'

And with that she stormed off in the direction of the cloakroom to retrieve her packed lunch. She waved and hooted down the corridor at John West, who she normally hates. 'Wait for me! Fancy a game of footie later?' Peter and I watched her run after a scared-looking John.

'Oh well, she's OK, then,' Peter said, looking back at me with a grim smile on his face. If Peter walked away now, that would be it. I would be officially all on my own for an entire hour while the rest of the school had the best time of their lives. It would probably go down in school history as the most fun lunch hour ever, no one noticing that I had quietly slunk into a corner of the school playground. I looked at Peter intensely, waiting to see what his decision would be. I didn't dare ask him to stick with me over lunch. I couldn't afford to reveal the *exact* level of desperate agony my stupid, angry behaviour had reduced me to.

'Come on,' he said after ages. 'It's cauliflower cheese today.'

'Yum-yum,' I said, then added, 'Thanks, Peter.'

'Don't be stupid,' he said, pushing me in the direction of the canteen. 'Anything to get out of a game of footie with Nikky.'

Lunch wasn't too bad, if you ignored the now-permanent sick feeling in my stomach. I couldn't actually *eat* anything, but at least Peter was there to give me silent support as I watched

Kate on the other side of the canteen. Sitting with Edward.

'Stop watching,' Peter told me, once I'd explained to him exactly why Kate and I had fallen out. But that was like telling an Xbox addict to walk away from the controller. It wasn't going to happen. And even though it was eating me up inside, I couldn't tear my eyes away from the picture of Kate enjoying being with Edward more than me. I may as well have been sticking needles into my eyeballs.

'You're only making yourself more miserable,' Peter scolded, stating the obvious.

'No choice,' I mumbled, refusing to look away.

As Edward prised open the slices of bread in his sandwich to show Kate the contents, I watched.

As Kate offered Edward her apple and grinned as he took a huge bite out of it, I watched.

And as they each took alternate sips from the carton of Ribena they were sharing, I watched.

SWALK

Then I craned my neck to see if there were actually oysters and caviar in their lunch boxes, because they were certainly behaving as though this was the most romantic meal of their lives. They were oblivious to the freckled boy sitting opposite them, who was chewing on a carrot and shamelessly watching their every move, and they were certainly oblivious to me.

'Get out of the way!' I hissed as a younger kid made the mistake of walking into my line of vision. I shoved him roughly to one side and didn't bother apologizing when his dinner tray clattered to the floor.

'Right. That's enough,' declared Peter, and he roughly dragged me to my feet, frogmarching me out of the canteen as I craned my head round, still desperate to see what Edward and Kate would do next. That was a mistake. As Peter peeled my fingers away from the doorframe I yelped with pain, causing Kate and half the canteen to look up. Kate and I caught each other's eyes. And even though it must have been obvious to her at that moment just how miserable I was she turned back to

SWALK

Edward, tossed her hair over her shoulder and leant in close to whisper something in his ear. Now I really couldn't watch any more. I trailed after Peter into the playground.

The rest of the day passed in a fog of pure misery and it seemed as though 3.30 would never arrive. But as everyone else rushed to pack their bags and get out of school, I hung back.

'Is everything OK, Emma?' asked Miss Cameron, when she noticed me lingering. It's not like me to hang around the classroom for a minute more than I have to.

'Yes, Miss,' I said limply.

'Are you sure?' she persisted, squinting at me over the top of her glasses.

'She's fine,' said a voice behind me as Peter put a hand on my shoulder and gently steered me towards the classroom door.

We walked home together in silence. By the time we reached the corner of Church Lane, all the other kids had already peeled off and gone into their separate houses and the two of us stood alone beneath the conker tree. 'Here we are again,' said Peter, stating the obvious for the second time that day.

I nodded, desperate to get back to the house for a reassuring hug from my mum. 'I've got to go,' I told him, feeling guilty that I was too strung out to behave better. Especially since he'd been such a good friend to me today.

'I understand,' he said. 'Your mum'll be worrying.'

When I got home I walked through every room of the house, looking for my mum. I found her in the back garden, taking washing down from the line. Of course, even this was a performance. Sheets were being dramatically launched into the linen basket, landing in crumpled heaps with no regard for next-door's cat, who had settled on top of the pile of freshly washed laundry.

I watched silently and by the time I traipsed after Mum back into the kitchen, the two of us still hadn't said a word to each other. Partly because Mum had her mouth full of clothes pegs. But as soon as we were in the kitchen Mum sank into a chair and pulled me to her. I didn't need asking to bury my face into her shoulder and begin to sob. Gently, Mum rocked us both from side to side, stroking my hair and making reassuring noises. And for once she was playing it down and not making a big scene. I have never needed a hug as much as I needed one right then.

Finally, I was able to stop crying and Mum pulled me on to her knee, even though I am far too big to be sitting on people's knees and haven't officially indulged in this practice for at least three years. But the good thing about home is that you never have to worry about your friends seeing you if you might be having a bit of a cuddle. Mum and I still hadn't said anything and I couldn't work out how she knew that I was so upset. Despite the badly crumpled pile of laundry sitting next to us, I began to think that perhaps my mum was better at being a mum than I thought.

'Kate's mum phoned,' she said.

'Oh,' I said. We sat in silence for a few moments longer and then Mum started again.

'Kate's terribly upset,' she told me gently, trying not to make too big a deal out of the fact that Kate being upset had quite a lot to do with me. I pointed at my own face and the recently dried tears in an extremely sarcastic

'Perhaps-I'm-upset-too' type way.

'OK, OK,' Mum shushed. 'But perhaps you should try to phone her later tonight. Once you've had a bath and calmed down. Don't let hurt pride stand between yourself and your friend, Emma. Look how miserable it's making you.'

I could see where Mum was coming from, but I couldn't even think about it any more. I was exhausted. 'I'm going to my room,' I mumbled, slipping off Mum's lap and walking up the stairs. As I shut my bedroom door I flopped on to the bed. 'Goodbye, world,' I muttered into the quilt. 'And good riddance.' I have never been so glad to get to the end of a day.

CHAPTER EIGHT

I didn't phone Kate that evening, and the next day at school we both sat facing the front of the class ignoring each other all over again. It gave me a serious case of neckache. An atmosphere of extreme unhappiness combined with barely restrained misery ruined every class. But hey. After a few days, you get used to these things.

Kate pranced around after Edward every lunchtime, and I clung to Peter with fragile gratitude. A bit like a wet dog who's just been let in and follows you round the house. Strangely, Peter didn't seem to mind.

In fact, once I'd got past how unhappy I was without Kate, it kind of made a nice change. I had to admit that there was something compelling about listening to a whole new set of stories and jokes that you've never heard before from someone other than your best friend. And it was intriguing to find out about the way someone else did things. For example, Peter wasn't like Kate and me, he didn't read the last paragraph of the book first. 'What's the point in that?' he'd ask, amazed. 'You're just ruining the story.'

'No, you're not,' I said. 'We've always done that.' But I wasn't so sure that I was right and Peter was wrong. Or if Peter had a sandwich at lunchtime, he would leave all the crusts till last. Like, why would you want to save up all those horrible crusts to eat in one go? Now, me, I wouldn't eat the crusts at all.

'Bizarre . . .' we'd marvel, shaking our heads at each other's plate.

Of course, as a backdrop to all this real-life drama, rehearsals for the play had now started in earnest. Every morning different cast members would be called out of class to join in with whatever scene Mr Taylor was running through. And as I got out of long multiplication for the third time that week, even I couldn't deny that being cast as Third Donkey still had something going for it.

Of course, the two leading actors had to be at pretty much every rehearsal. All eyes were glued on Kate and Edward. Mr Taylor would watch the two of them up on stage together, hugging himself as though he couldn't believe his luck. It wasn't just that Edward had the confidence to swagger through his role as Samson. Or even that Kate was word-perfect from day one. The two of them clicked. They didn't need a prompter, they didn't need crosses on the stage to show them where to stand, and it was a waste of time Mr Taylor trying to 'direct' them. They were born to be on the stage together and the rest of us may as well have just packed up our bags and gone home.

In the meantime, I sat glumly and watched. It was the second Friday since rehearsals had started and I was in my usual place offstage, watching the action, when Peter appeared at my side, sitting down on the canvas chair next to me. We sat in silence for a few minutes.

Slowly, he leant over and whispered in my ear, 'You OK?'

Sternly I shushed him.

'We're not allowed to talk while people are acting,' I hissed. I edged over in my seat so that my back was partially to him. I was busy watching my best friend being extremely happy with someone else, and didn't need any interruptions. He dragged his chair closer.

'Only, I wanted to speak to you about something, Emma.'

I tutted loudly. A group of kids sat on the floor in front of us turned round as one and raised their index fingers to their lips, frowning at us. Peter grabbed hold of my hand and jerked his head towards the cloakroom. I got up and followed him, skulking past the stage just as Kate and Edward launched into another of their duets.

The cloakroom is probably my favourite place in the whole school. It's always that little bit too hot in there, and the crowded rows of empty jackets, anoraks and coats make it kind of cosy. It's a good place to hide when you don't want to see anyone.

Peter and I sat on one of the narrow wooden benches and leant back against the racks, half disappearing into the thick folds of coats. Peter jangled a foot against the metal grille underneath the bench. All I could see of him was the tip of his nose.

'When are you going to make it up with Kate?' he asked eventually.

I started whistling off-tune, trying to pretend that I hadn't heard him. A hand reached out from behind a grubby duffel coat and slapped over my mouth.

'Thash verr ude!' I tried to protest from behind his clammy palm.

'Did you hear what I said?' he asked firmly. I peeled his fingers away and nodded my head, even though I knew he couldn't see me. He took his hand back and wiped it surreptitiously on the leg of his trousers.

'That's better. I'll begin again. When. Are. You. Going. To. Make. Friends?' This wasn't like Peter at all. He was usually so laid-back.

'What's with *you*?' I asked, bewildered.

Peter sighed loudly. 'I'm sick of this whole situation. It's gone on long enough,' he said. 'You're not speaking to Kate, Kate's not speaking to you, I'm constantly trying to act as peacemaker and Nikky's running out of people to force into playing football with her. It's horrible and I want it to stop. And . . .' Here he hesitated. He gulped loudly and plunged on. 'You're the person who started all this and you're the person who should finish it. Now.'

I kicked my heel against the metal grille. 'For your information, Mr High and Mighty, all of this is not just my fault. On more than one occasion Miss Perfect stood me up to be with Edward.'

'She didn't let you know she couldn't make it?' Peter asked.

My eyes fell to the ground. 'Well, yes. OK, she did let me know. But that didn't stop it hurting my feelings!' I said, exasperated.

'I'm sure it must have. I'd have been the same. But still . . . someone's got to be big enough to end this, Emma.'

'Gordon Bennett!' I exclaimed. 'If it'll make you *feel* any better!' Then I tutted loudly. Peter didn't say anything. He knew I had to pretend I was doing this for his sake. 'I mean, I wouldn't want you to get your knickers in a twist or anything! OK, first chance I get, I'll grapple Edward out of the way and have a word with Kate.'

'Erm, if you want a piece of advice, I'd do less of the Edward-grappling,' Peter interrupted. I snorted. 'I mean, this is part of the whole problem, isn't it? You've got to accept that Kate's got a new friend.' I peered round the duffel coat to glare at him, but Peter returned my gaze defiantly.

'Don't you mean *boyfriend*?' I asked menacingly.

Peter shrugged his shoulders. 'Whatever,' he said, as though he genuinely didn't care one way or another. Which he probably didn't. After all, it wasn't him who had recently been Betrayed by a Best Friend. I thumped a PE kit on to the floor.

'She still likes you, and that's never going to go away. Unless you make it.' Peter finished.

I leant back and wound someone else's scarf round my neck as I thought this over. I sniffed it thoughtfully. I hated to admit it, but Peter had a point.

☆ ☆ ☆

I had to choose my moment carefully. I was hoping to sort things out with Kate without any witnesses. But in the end, I didn't have much choice. The next morning, as I came out of the house wiping the last of the cornflakes from my mouth, I stumbled over something on the doorstep and nearly fell headlong into Sam's pram, which was parked outside by the kitchen window. I looked over my shoulder at the back door, where a large object called Nikky was glaring at the postman in a silent dare to come any nearer. I picked myself up.

'How long have you been there?' I asked in confusion. It was one of those autumn mornings where the sun is really bright, but the cold can seep into your bones and any normal person sitting on a doorstep would have been frozen.

'Oh, long enough,' she replied enigmatically, unfolding her long legs as she stood up.

I gulped. 'What do you want?'

The postman edged nervously past the two of us, Mum waving gaily at him through the steamed-up kitchen window, a soapy dishcloth in one hand.

Nikky didn't answer. She stared at me. I tried

to stare back. Eventually she turned to walk down the drive and I knew I was expected to follow her. As we stepped out on to the pavement she started talking.

'I hear Peter had his little chat with you yesterday.'

'Oh, so this was all planned between you, was it?' I asked.

'Well, if you think the two of us *caring* is a conspiracy, then I guess you've every right to be so flippin' prickly,' she retorted, quickening her step.

I stumbled to keep up with her. 'All right, all right,' I blustered, hoping she'd accept that as an apology. As we reached Church Lane Nikky slowed down to lean against the conker tree.

'What're you doing?' I asked. 'We've only got ten minutes before school. And you know what Miss Cameron is like in the mornings.'

Once again Nikky didn't answer, but inspected her nails closely, which struck me as odd when you consider she doesn't usually put much store by personal grooming.

'What's going on?' I asked.

Nikky looked up and past me, peering into the distance. Then, 'Here they come now.'

'Here who come . . . ?' I started to ask, turning to look over my shoulder. I turned back to face Nikky sharply. 'No, come on. This isn't fair.'

'You made a promise to Peter,' said Nikky, looking stern. 'And I'm here to make sure you keep it.' She swung one leg nonchalantly, kicking soggy leaves over the pavement as I turned back to watch the slow and inevitable approach of Kate and Edward.

Kate was laughing. Her breath came out in big smoky clouds in the crisp air. Edward was watching her, enjoying the effect his jokes were having on *my* friend. I'd read about the red mist of anger in those murder mystery books Mum *thinks* she's banned me from reading, but now I was experiencing the real thing for myself. I couldn't speak, my hands were clenched, and for the first time in my life I was considering actual physical violence. Bearing in mind what a coward I usually am, that was saying a lot.

Would the authorities put a young girl like me in jail for thumping a stupid friend-stealer like Edward? Surely not.

Nikky was still watching me. I was kind of hoping that she'd throw herself between Edward and me at the last minute to save me from myself, but from the look on her face I knew that wasn't going to happen. It suddenly dawned on me that this was Nikky's way of seeing if I was going to carry out my promise to Peter. 'You're testing me, aren't you?' I asked through gritted teeth, without taking my eyes off Kate and Edward.

'You might say that,' she replied, with a sadist's thin smile. 'I couldn't possibly comment. Anyway, no time to chat now. They're almost here.'

I looked round again to see them crossing the road. Kate actually half skipped. Then her skip slowed to a reluctant walk as she spotted Nikky and me.

SWALK

'Hi,' Kate ventured, looking over at Edward nervously. She was obviously expecting trouble.

'Hi!' replied Nikky brightly. I just stood there, looking and feeling like a complete idiot. One of my knees was jangling nervously and I didn't seem to be able to stop it. I clamped a hand to my leg and forced a smile on to my face.

'Hi, Kate,' I started, then looked at Edward. 'Hi, Edward,' I finished. He smiled back at me. I expected the red mist to descend again, but it was only faintly pinkish this time. It was looking like I might just be able to pull this off. Then I'm not sure, but I could have sworn I saw Nikky nodding at Edward as if to prompt him.

'Oh, Emma,' he suddenly blurted out. 'I was just thinking we should all go to the cafe some time after school. Whaddya reckon? This afternoon?'

His voice came out in a rushed monotone, as though he was running through something rehearsed, but Nikky looked satisfied. My knee started trembling again. I looked down at the pavement and struggled with my conscience. Well, I say conscience. It's not like I was having a moral battle with myself. I knew I had to agree to this in order to make friends with Kate, but I also knew I was being set up. I mean, Edward and I had never spoken to each other before in our lives and suddenly he's inviting me to the cafe? Peter, Nikky and Edward had arranged this whole thing between them. All I had to do to get my best friend back was pretend I hadn't cottoned on. I wasn't sure if the words were going to stick in my throat, but eventually I heard myself say, 'Yeah, OK. I think I could force a milkshake down.' I tried out a smile and I *think* my mouth opened in a grin. But I didn't feel anything like a smile going on inside. Still, Kate seemed convinced and I realized she was smiling back at me. So was Edward. Nikky sagely nodded her head in approval. We were one big happy family by the looks of things.

☆ ☆ ☆

After school I explained to Mum that that morning I'd had a touching reconciliation with my best friend that deserved a celebratory milkshake at the cafe with my mates. 'Just don't be late home,' she'd called after me.

Dot's Cafe is the kind that has faded plastic-covered menus and chairs fixed to the floor. But Dot doesn't seem to mind a load of screaming kids crammed into the booths every afternoon. Don't ask me how it began, but this is the place to hang out when you're not at school. I think every town has a Dot's Cafe.

Peter and I had squeezed ourselves into a booth, while Kate and Edward were at the counter ordering five frothy milkshakes and don't hold the sugar. Nikky was outside bending some old bloke's ear for daring to hold open the door for her.

'Do you want me to help you learn your lines? Read them out loud, like?' Peter offered as we waited for our friends to join us.

'Give over,' I snorted. 'I only have five lines and they're all the same. So I'll risk not practising them today.' He looked disappointed.

'Would you like me to help you with your lines?' I offered, hoping he'd accept the olive branch. I'd only just made it up with Kate, I wasn't in the mood to lose another friend just now.

He smiled grimly. 'Well, plebs don't have that much to say in the play either. In fact, I don't have any lines to remember.' We looked at each other and laughed. At least there was someone else in the same boat as me.

Then he reached his hand out across the table. It hovered over mine for a few seconds and I watched it, wondering what on earth he was doing. Peter stared at his hand too, watching it shake until Nikky burst through the cafe door and Peter hastily grabbed a menu, studying it like his life depended on memorizing every type of herbal tea.

'Had enough of the Revolution for the afternoon?' I asked Nikky in a wobbly voice, still feeling a bit funny about Peter's strange behaviour, while he still stared determinedly at the menu. Nikky just grinned.

'Come on, you two!' she shouted over to Kate and Edward. 'I need my sugar fix.'

They wandered over to our booth, each of them carefully balancing a tray. Edward handed out the tall glasses, straws floating perilously on the surface of the frothy milkshakes. He snuck into the booth next to me and I had no option but to budge over and make room for him. I tried to be shocked by his nerve, but my heart wasn't in it. I tested out a couple of my better jokes on him and he had the decency to laugh. Perhaps he wasn't so bad after all.

After my second milkshake I got up to go to the loo, and when I came back I made a point of going to sit next to Kate. After all, we may have made friends again, but we hadn't had much time to talk yet. Edward was over on the other side of the table, watching us carefully, but after the past few days I don't suppose I could blame him for being protective of Kate.

Fortunately for me, there were still lots of secrets I had with Kate that hopefully he would never know about. For one thing, we had our own secret language. Rubbing your nose meant 'Let's get out of here.' Tugging your left ear lobe meant 'Rescue me from this idiot.' We'd invented hundreds of these secret signals. It was just a struggle to remember them all. Sometimes Kate and I got confused and one of us would mistake a 'Meet you outside,' for a 'See you in the kitchen,' so that Kate waited outside, listlessly kicking the wall while I perched on a kitchen stool wondering why I was sitting like a lemon on my own. But it made us laugh. And then there was the extra-special secret code. It was a bit complicated, but it went like this: you reached down to tighten the lace on your left trainer, then you pulled up and straightened both socks (first left, then right), touched four different points on your face (which I can't tell you because then I'd have to kill you) and finished with a scratch to the right armpit.

Nikky and Peter were listening, open-mouthed, to some story Edward was telling them about his summer holiday in Florida, and Kate was smiling and listening too. Gently, I nudged Kate and then bent down to tighten my left shoelace, hoping more than anything that Kate was watching me. It was difficult to tell, what with my head being stuck under the counter. I straightened both socks in strict order and then sat up awkwardly. The noise of Edward talking had faded into a dull background drone. He hadn't a clue. Carefully, I touched my face four times and then gave my right armpit a really good scratch. Finally, I turned round to look at Kate. My Best Friend. She was grinning from ear to ear. 'Thank you,' she whispered, 'I'm so glad to have you back,' and we gave each other a big hug.

'Me too,' I whispered in reply.

And what had that secret signal said? 'Best Friends Forever, Never To Be Parted.'

CHAPTER NINE

Now that we were best friends again Kate was really keen that Edward and I got on, and I tried to show willing. This meant that suddenly, there were three of us sitting on the school steps at break time, which was a bit cosy, and people kept knocking into me with their knees as they tried to get by. Every time another pair of bony legs pushed past me I'd smile thinly at Kate and Edward, and we'd all shove along a bit closer to try and make more room. But there really wasn't enough space for three backsides on that step. Sooner or later, I'd find an excuse to wander off and Kate and Edward would wave me goodbye. As I reached the corner of the school building I'd pause to look back at them, but they'd already be deep in conversation.

On Friday Mr Taylor called an emergency meeting of the cast and choir. When he walked into the assembly hall, he looked like a defeated man. His shoulders sagged under his misshapen jacket but most important of all – he'd even forgotten to put a horrible tie on. We all knew something must be seriously wrong.

He stood before us and allowed his gaze to travel across our faces, looking for all the world like he just didn't care any more. He cleared his throat.

'I've asked you here because the Big Day is fast approaching. We've all been working hard to get this play ready, but I'm afraid drastic improvement is needed if we're not going to look like a group of complete idiots.' I was surprised – teachers weren't usually this honest. But Mr Taylor had a point. The two lead actors were confident and impressive – everything you'd want from your stars. But as for the rest of us . . . half the cast still didn't know all their lines and the choir was becoming more and more of a liability as they failed to get through even one song without badly losing the tune.

'The truth is, I want us all to have fun. But word's come from above that this play has to be as good as it can be.' We could all sense something bad coming. Peter tried to give my hand a comforting squeeze and I let him.

'So it's been decided that Mrs Rogers is going to become a bit more involved. She'll start with the choir. I hope you'll give her all the support you can and do everything she tells you.' He walked over to the double doors, grasped the brass handles and swung them open. In walked Mrs Rogers.

She wasted no time at all.

'Now, then, choir. Form a group, that's right – quick, quick! I want you to run through the first song of the play: "Delightful Delilah". I shall walk among you as you're singing and if I tap you on the head, I want you to leave the group and go back to your classroom. We need to weed out all the weak voices in this choir and really get things into shape. Now don't worry, this isn't personal – it's just, erm, re-organization.' She smiled through gritted teeth as the choir looked stony-faced back at her.

She cleared her throat. 'And a one, two, three, four . . .' The choir hesitantly started singing and their voices continued to wobble as Mrs Rogers walked from person to person, bending her head to the voice of each member as she passed. It didn't take long for sharp taps to start and one by one, singers peeled away from the group and walked slowly out of the assembly hall.

I couldn't believe what I was seeing. I looked over to Mr Taylor, but he wasn't watching. He was pretending to repair one of the papier mâché cacti. Eventually, 'Delightful Delilah' stumbled to a halt and Mrs Rogers seemed satisfied. Ten choir members were left standing.

'Hmm, well, we're not left with much. You're all going to have to work very hard at voice projection. But better to have a few strong voices than a load of . . .' She trailed off.

Mr Taylor looked round unhappily, and Mrs Rogers raised her eyebrows in a 'Well?' manner. He cleared his throat and just about managed to look us in the face.

'OK, now that's sorted, let's get on with Act Three, shall we?'

The cast looked at each other nervously. Act Three was Dave Pilchard's one and only scene, but he'd already gained a reputation as a bit of a loose cannon onstage. None of us were sure Mrs Rogers would be able to tolerate his antics. But Dave enjoyed an audience – even a hostile one – and I was pretty sure he wouldn't let Mrs Rogers prevent him from playing up . . .

Act Three, Scene One

    Innkeeper: Come on now, drink up! I want you all out of here.
    Drinker: Yeah, yeah, just five more minutes.
    Innkeeper: Now, I mean it . . . whoa . . . whoa . . . aarghhh!

(*Dave Pilchard falls off edge of stage, exiting stage left.*)

    Drinker: Where's he gone? (*Looking around confused.*)

Innkeeper: Here I am, here I am. A bit too much of the Old Testament ale, if you'll excuse me.

(*Dave Pilchard climbs back on to stage, enter stage right.*)

Drinker: Oh, erm. Well, as I was saying . . . just five more minutes?

(*Appeals to Mr Taylor.*)

Innkeeper: Listen, mate. You'll sling your hook quick sharp or I'll be over this bar and slinging a bunch of fives in your direction.
Drinker (appealing to Mr Taylor): That's not in the script!

(*Drinker storms off stage in disgust.*)

Dave called this improvisation. I wasn't sure what Mrs Rogers would call it. As he started yet another comedy routine, staggering off towards the edge of the stage, she leapt up on to the wooden platform and ran after him, catching him by his school tie and pulling him round to face her, a terrifying glint in her eye. Then she let rip.

'What on earth do you think you're doing?' she screeched. 'That is the most amateur, lazy performance I've ever seen. Call yourself an actor?'

You could see Dave's bravado begin to slip. 'Hey, I was just getting into the role . . .' he began.

'Don't you interrupt me!' She looked like she was going to explode with rage. I didn't think teachers were allowed to behave like this any more. But clearly Mrs Rogers was.

'I want you to vacate this stage immediately. Your services are no longer required.'

Mr Taylor tried to interject, but she threw him a warning look. He slunk away.

Mrs Rogers grabbed Dave Pilchard's shoulders, swung him round and gave him a rough shove that left him in no doubt that he was facing his final exit from the stage. He stumbled down and walked quickly out of the assembly hall, Mrs Rogers watching him sternly. As he flung open the double doors, he turned back one last time to throw a scowl at Mrs Rogers. But she didn't take any notice.

She'd already turned her back on Dave and was talking to Kate about her next scene. Dave shook his head menacingly and let the doors slam behind him.

As we walked out of school at the end of the day, Kate and I were pretty quiet. I mean, what with the day's events, we had a lot to think about. But as we approached the school gates Kate slowed down. She was staring hard at the ground.

'Are you sure you're OK about Edward these days?' she started.

I couldn't help a sigh escaping. I was tired, I was fed up and just about the last person I felt like talking about was Edward Ponsford.

'Of course I'm OK about it,' I said, my voice brittle. 'Why shouldn't I be?'

Kate peered closely at me. 'I don't know. It's just that you don't *seem* that happy,' she said.

I couldn't help sighing again. 'I try, don't I?' I complained, my patience running out.

'So you have to make an effort, then?' Kate asked.

Leave me be! I thought to myself. But talk of the devil, there was Bible Boy himself, waiting for us by the school gates.

'Look, we can talk about this if you want to. But do we have to do it in front of him?' I asked.

Kate looked up and spotted Edward. I could see her bristle. 'And who's "him"? Can't you use his name?'

'Oh, I could. If I wanted to,' I replied. I allowed the unspoken insult to Edward to hang in the air between us, but I could see I'd made a mistake. 'Are you coming or what?' I asked in a quieter voice, panic seeping through me.

SWALK

'It's OK, you go on ahead,' Kate replied firmly.

'Suit yourself!' I said, trying to sound nonchalant, and turned away, angry tears filling my eyes.

☆ ☆ ☆

When I got home Dad was up to his eyeballs in paperwork at the kitchen table and absentmindedly gave me a kiss over the lid of his laptop. Mum was trying to get tea ready, struggling with the can-opener to get into a Fray Bentos tin. I slumped into a chair and watched her. She carried on working in silence for a few minutes until she noticed she was being watched. 'How were rehearsals?' she asked vaguely.

I shrugged my shoulders. 'Well, Mrs Rogers's taken over and sacked half the choir,' I managed to say.

'Oh, that woman!' tutted my mum, giving the can an angry shake.

'And Kate's fallen out with me again.'

The smile slid off Mum's face. 'Oh, darling!' she gushed. 'What's happened this time?'

'Oh, just my big mouth again. The usual.' Dad stopped thumping the laptop's keyboard and peered at me over the top of his half-moon glasses, looking worried. Everything went blurry as I struggled not to cry, but I could see Mum walking over towards me looking concerned. I opened my mouth to say something but before I could, a desperate howl escaped my mouth. I must have been under more of a strain than I'd realized over the past few weeks. (And I'm not just talking about the heavy responsibility of bringing an Old Testament donkey to life on stage.) Dad hastily pushed back his chair as Mum brushed past him, the two of them rushing to get to me first. I almost feared for my life as four arms flung themselves round me and I was manhandled into a group hug. They may have been squeezing the life out of me, but it felt good.

☆ ☆ ☆

I managed to stop crying long enough to eat my tea, Mum and Dad watching me anxiously as I put another forkful of dry pie and lumpy gravy into my mouth. They waited until I'd finished eating before forcing me to talk about things.

The three of us walked into the lounge together, Mum carrying Sam, and Dad leading me by the hand. I didn't much like having my hand held, but after my little performance I figured I ought to humour him. We sat in a row on the sofa and for one of the few times I could remember in our family's history, the TV was switched off.

'OK,' said Mum. 'Start at the beginning.'

So I took a deep breath and told them everything. All about Edward and how I felt abandoned by Kate. How I'd tried to be friends with both of them, but still felt pushed out. I tried to gloss over some of the details of my recent behaviour, but Mum forced me to tell them everything.

'It's the only way we can help you, sweet-heart,' she said. It took a long time and when I'd finished there was a sombre pause. Mum and Dad looked at each other over the top of my head, while Sam giggled to himself as he fiddled with the laces of my trainers.

Dad coughed quietly into his hand, which I think meant he wanted to say something. Dad's not quite like Mum. She's always happy to take centre stage with her opinions, but Dad is a bit more slow in coming forward. It doesn't bother me. In fact, sometimes I prefer it. It means you're actually interested in hearing what he thinks when he does have something to say. Mum and I sat back carefully and folded our arms. We didn't want to do or say anything to scare Dad off his moment. Finally, he opened his mouth to speak.

'The thing is, Emma, you've got yourself into a pickle and no mistake. But that isn't to say that things can't be mended. Let me tell you this, I've watched from the wings countless times as your mum's taken her bows to rapturous applause.'

I slid a glance at Mum, who sat up a bit more straight. It must have been killing her to keep quiet.

'But do you know who's there the next day, and the next week, and the next year? Me. And where are all those people who were fawning over your mother? They've gone back to their own lives and they've forgotten to keep telling her how wonderful she is. And that's why, after your family, your friends are so important, Emma. They are the only permanent fan club you'll ever have. Friends like Kate don't come along very often, and you owe it to yourself to make things right again with her.'

A suppressed sob came from the direction of

my mother, and Dad and I caught each other's eye in amusement. It was Mum's turn now and she threw her arms round my dad. '"Thou art as wise as thou art beautiful",' she declared solemnly, holding my dad's face between her hands.

Dad's eyes shifted nervously from side to side, as though he were looking for the person who was going to come and rescue him. Then he looked back at Mum. 'Erm, *A Midsummer Night's Dream*?' he asked, hesitantly.

'Darling, yes. Can't you remember me in Act Three? It was one of my best moments.'

'Yes, yes, of course,' Dad said quickly, prising Mum's fingers from his cheeks and putting them delicately back in her lap.

I sighed. Mum and Dad were right, but I was still feeling hard done by. 'I wouldn't mind so much, but Kate's been really horrible to me too, you know,' I couldn't help blurting out.

'*Really* horrible?' asked Mum gently, in a tone of voice that suggested she knew Kate couldn't be really horrible if she tried.

'OK, not *really* horrible.'

'Good thing it's the weekend. That'll give Kate time to calm down and you time to work out how you're going to make things up to her, eh?' Dad said, surreptitiously sneaking a glance at his watch.

'Don't worry, you can put the telly back on now,' I told him. From long and bitter experience, I knew it wasn't a good idea to make Dad miss the business news.

'And what are you going to do?' asked Mum as Dad eagerly reached for the remote.

I shook my head. 'I have no idea,' I replied. 'But I know one thing. It's going to have to be good.'

CHAPTER TEN

Time can do funny things. Teachers tell you that everything is down to seconds, minutes and hours. But have you ever noticed how fast an hour goes when you know it's nearly time to go to bed? Or how slow a minute can seem when it's the last class of the day? It's not as straightforward as some people make out. And boy, did that weekend drag its heels. Part of me didn't want Monday morning to arrive at all. But another part just wanted the worst behind me. It was also the loneliest weekend I'd had in a while and the phone never rang for me – though Dad was constantly taking calls from clients phoning to ask about tax returns, VAT receipts and other boring, grown-up stuff. It's a sad day when your dad is more popular than you.

So I had a lot of spare time in which to think about things. But instead of coming up with a solution, all I kept coming back to was that so far the rules of my life had been very simple:

The Rules of Emma's Life
Kate is my best friend.
I am Kate's best friend.
Boys are boring.

It wasn't complicated and I didn't have to think about it. This was just the way life was. But things had changed and suddenly all the rules of life were looking a bit wobbly and unsure of themselves. I didn't like it one bit, but I also didn't have much choice.

Eventually, Monday morning dawned. I know it dawned, because I was up early enough to see the sun rise. When I'm anxious, I wake up early. When my mum's anxious, she stays in bed and sends Dad out for doughnuts. People are just different – something I was beginning to learn. But as I said, I was up early that Monday morning. I hadn't the heart for breakfast, but Mum forced some burnt toast into my hand as she pushed me out of the front door with a hug and a wink.

'Everything will be all right, you'll see,' she said, crouching down so that we were face to face.

'You're only saying that. How do you know?' I asked sulkily.

'Because you'll make it all right. I have faith in you.' I harrumphed and shifted my backpack further up on my shoulder, but I was secretly glad for the support.

'Here goes nothing,' I muttered as I walked off down the drive. I didn't look back at Mum as I turned the corner. I was worried that if I did, I might never make it to school.

☆ ☆ ☆

That morning's rehearsals were painful to watch. Of course, it just had to be one of the key scenes between Samson and Delilah . . .

Act Four, Scene Five
Prison interior. Delilah visiting Samson as he languishes behind bars.

Samson: Come to gloat, have you?

Delilah: Erm, well, how shall I put it? Yes!

Samson: How could you? All I ever did was love you, and you betrayed me.

Delilah: Honey, you've got to take the rough with the smooth. I mean, come on. You don't think I actually, you know, liked you, did you? You're a Nazirite, for heaven's sake!

Samson: Don't you feel in the slightest bit guilty?

Delilah: With a nice bag of gold back home? I don't think so. You should know better by now, Samson. It's dog eat dog in this world.

Delilah turns to the audience and begins singing:

I'm an old-fashioned girl from the
  Bible
A lesson in all the world's ills
So sue me for being a good-time girl
I'm in it for money and thrills!

I'm an old-fashioned girl from the
  Bible
Girl Power is nothing new
Old Testament blokes just bore me to
  tears:
they really don't have a clue.

So show me a fine time, and give me
  your cash
I'm a good girl sometimes, if I choose
But I'd rather be bad and have a good
  laugh
than suffer from the Bible Girl Blues.

Both Kate and Edward were obviously enjoying themselves. Kate didn't look as though she'd wasted a moment of the weekend worrying about me, and her cheeks shone rosily as she sang her heart out, sashaying across the stage. The script asked Delilah to look out into the audience, making eye contact as she sang this song, but her gaze glided over me as she smiled at all the other schoolkids watching her in silent awe.

SWALK

I had no idea what I was going to do. I watched miserably from the side of the stage as Kate seemed to ignore me effortlessly. I sank deeper into my chair as Edward, in his Samson toga, joined Kate on stage and they began another of their key scenes. Mr Taylor stood in front of the stage, a dog-eared copy of the script in his hand, mouthing the words silently as the action unfolded. It was clear that our teacher was a frustrated actor, dearly wishing he'd been able to choose himself to play Samson.

I guess that's why Mr Taylor didn't notice what was happening that morning. He was too caught up in the play. I, on the other hand, would rather have been looking anywhere than at Samson as he knelt at Delilah's feet, imploring her not to force him to confess the secret of his strength. Kate was gazing down at Edward, entranced, so it was no surprise she didn't see what was coming either.

Dave Pilchard had been keeping a very low profile ever since Mrs Rogers had unceremoniously sacked him from the play. The rest of us had been so caught up in rehearsals that we hadn't really noticed his absence – not just from the play but from the whole school scene. Which now I came to think of it, was a mistake. We should have noticed that one of the biggest show-offs in school wasn't showing off. It had alarm bells written all over it. But looking back, I guess we should also have stopped to think about how Dave Pilchard was feeling after his sensational eviction. Because as it turns out, even comedians like Dave Pilchard have a sensitive side. And it was about to be revealed in dramatic style.

I saw him emerge from behind the scenery and at first, I thought he was up to another of his stupid pranks. But there was something about the way he was crouched over that didn't seem right. Dave usually walks with his shoulders thrown back and chest proudly thrust out. The way people do when they think they're fantastic. But as his eyes focused on Kate I saw his eyelids narrow. It wasn't a nice look. That's when I spotted the bucket of water hanging heavily from his hand.

Dave started to sprint across the stage and after that everything happened very quickly.

Edward, who was the only one to see what was coming, leapt backwards off the stage, into Mr Taylor's arms, and the two of them crumpled in a heap on the floor, Mr Taylor yelping with pain. Mrs Rogers turned round sharply from the piano, looking furious, but was too far from the stage to do anything. Kate looked behind her in puzzlement, at which point I suddenly realized what was happening and leapt from my seat up on to the stage.

Dave lunged towards Kate, letting out a battle cry of startling volume, and swinging the bucket of icy-looking water towards her. I threw my whole body at his legs, rugby-tackling him to the floor. The bucket slipped from his grasp and tipped over the edge of the stage, drenching Mr Taylor and Edward while Dave struggled beneath me, protesting loudly with the kind of language that makes hardened teachers wince. It was pretty difficult to keep him down, but fortunately Nikky joined me at that point, sitting self-importantly on Dave's stomach. I sat back on my heels to catch my breath, and looked around me at the chaotic scene. Dave, who was still pinned down, was red in the face and furious. Mr Taylor was peeking over the edge of the stage, wringing the water from his nylon tie and Kate stood listlessly, her arms drooping by her side, her mouth open in a tiny 'o' of shock.

Of course, Mrs Rogers was over in a flash. She came thumping up behind me and dragged Dave to his feet, pushing Nikky out of the way.

No one pushed Nikky around and Mrs Rogers should have known that. But just as Nikky was about to protest, Peter arrived by her side and gave her a congratulatory thump on the arm – which seemed to make her feel better.

'Boy! What on earth did you think you were doing?' demanded Mrs Rogers, sounding even more scary than normal.

Dave tried to wriggle out of her hold, but she tightened her grasp until he looked as though he was in danger of strangling himself if he didn't stop struggling. Eventually he gave up and slumped inside the shoulders of his school blazer.

'Nuffink,' he eventually mumbled under his breath.

'Speak up, boy!' shrieked Mrs Rogers, giving

him another shake before releasing her grip on him. 'Explain yourself.'

'I was trying to sabotage the play. I thought if Kate slipped and broke something crucial, like one of her perfect legs, you'd have to abandon the whole show. Serve you right for leaving me out.'

Peter and I looked at each other, shocked. The entire hall had fallen into deathly silence as we realized we were witnessing some real-life drama in our very own school. This beat *EastEnders* any day of the week.

'That is the most ridiculous thing I have ever heard,' guffawed Mrs Rogers cruelly. 'Look at you. Do you honestly think you could pull something like that off?'

The atmosphere had started to become uncomfortable and I don't think any of us enjoyed seeing Dave humiliated in this way. But while Mrs Rogers had been rattling Dave Pilchard, Mr Taylor had quietly and damply got to his feet. We all looked at him as he stood dripping on to the hall floor and knew that something big was going to happen. It was like watching the Incredible Hulk when his skin turns green and his shirt rips open. OK, so Mr

Taylor's muscles weren't exactly rippling – that could never happen – but he definitely looked very angry. Mrs Rogers noticed that everyone's attention had been drawn somewhere else and, still restraining Dave Pilchard with one angry fist, turned round to look at Mr Taylor. As her gaze settled on Mr Taylor's face I swear I saw a nervous tic start in her eye.

Mr Taylor leapt up on to the stage and braced himself before his colleague. 'Could we have a word in the staffroom, Mrs Rogers?' he asked, his voice trembling with anger.

The tic in her eye worsened. 'If you wish,' she replied, before releasing Dave and walking rigidly towards the staffroom door, not bothering to see if Mr Taylor was following her.

'Take a five-minute break,' Mr Taylor told us, without taking his eyes off Mrs Rogers. Then he strode after her.

The rest of us looked round at each other, wondering who would be the first to break the silence.

'What do you think they're doing in there?' I asked finally.

Nikky shook her head solemnly. 'I don't

know, but I wouldn't like to be Mrs Rogers. Not with the look on Mr Taylor's face.'

All of us jumped in the air when the staffroom door was flung open exactly five minutes later. We hadn't heard a single raised voice, but Mrs Rogers' face as she emerged was stony. Without sparing us a glance she stepped out into the playground and walked towards her car. Mr Taylor stood watching through the windows on the far side of the hall as we all tried to peer round him.

Silent clouds of exhaust formed as she edged her car slowly out of the car park and round the corner. Once she'd disappeared from view we all let out a spontaneous cheer of relief and delight. Mr Taylor visibly swelled with pride. For the first time ever, I felt a glimmer of respect for him. He turned round to us all and looked fit to burst. After all, it took an extraordinary person to stand up to Mrs Rogers, we all knew that.

'Ahem, well. Erm . . .' Mr Taylor began hesitantly, as if overwhelmed by his own show of bravery. 'The show must, you know . . .'

'Go on, sir?' asked the smallest of the Scott twins, helping him out.

'That's right, Emily. Come on, everyone. Back to Scene Three.'

And with that we all wandered slowly back towards the school stage.

I tried to settle inconspicuously into my chair, but no such luck. People crowded round to congratulate me on my brilliant rugby tackle, and Mr Inglethorp, the care-taker, stood at the back of the crowd that was forming round me, shaking his head in ever-increasing wonderment.

'Brilliant,' he kept saying over and over. 'Ruddy brilliant.'

I couldn't help laughing. I wasn't feeling nervous or anything, just a little bit proud of myself for once.

Someone pushed their way to the front of the crowd. Someone with long blonde hair hidden beneath a dark Delilah wig. As everyone else chattered and pointed at me, Kate didn't say anything but slowly bent down to tie a lace on an imaginary trainer. (Apparently, Nike wasn't around in the time of the Old

Testament.) She straightened two imaginary socks, left then right, touched her face four times and finally scratched her armpit through the toga she was wearing. It wasn't the most dignified thing I'd ever seen her do, but in our secret code it spoke volumes. I stood up out of my chair and linked arms with my best friend.

'Clear the way, please,' Kate announced. 'Emma and I have somewhere to be.' And with that we walked out of the hall and into the cloakroom. We turned to face each other, both of us blushing and struggling to meet each other's eye. 'I haven't got long, we've got to crack on with Act Two,' Kate said. 'But thanks a lot.' Before I had time to reply we heard Mr Taylor calling out Kate's name.

'You'd better get going,' I said.

Kate gave me a friendly hair tug. 'Where would I be without you?'

'Wet?' I suggested.

By the end of rehearsals that day we were shattered, but the play was really starting to come together. Most of the cast even managed to remember their lines, now that they didn't have Mrs Rogers constantly shouting at them. For the first time I think all of us – including Mr Taylor – dared to believe we could actually pull this off.

As I sat on the edge of the stage and studied the last small puddle of water left from Dave's dramatic entrance that afternoon, I realized that someone was standing behind me. I looked over my shoulder and saw that Kate had jumped down from the stage and was perching there. She shuffled her Delilah wig nervously in her hands.

'Emma, I didn't have enough time to say this before. But I just wanted to say . . . well, sorry for being such a bad friend lately.'

'What do you mean?' I asked, confused. I thought *I* was the one who'd been in the wrong.

'Well, it's tricky getting to know new friends, and not leaving out your old ones.' She paused, then took a deep breath. 'I didn't know what to do. So I didn't do anything. I'm really sorry, Emma. Can we still be friends?' She lowered her head so that her chin was nearly touching her chest and I had to strain to hear what she was saying.

I hadn't been expecting this. All along I'd assumed this whole mess had been my fault and it had never occurred to me that Kate and I might *share* the blame. Could it be . . . was it really . . . might I dare think that . . . Kate wasn't so perfect after all? I carefully picked a splinter of wood out of the stage floor while choosing what to say. I decided to come clean.

'Oh, look, I wasn't helping things either, was I? I haven't taken it very well. But you know what I'm like. I get so het up about things, and we've always been best friends. I knew I'd have to share you one day. So when you got together with Edward, I just panicked. But I'll always be your friend, if you still want that?'

There was a beat's silence and then Kate looked up at me. She put an arm round my shoulders and hugged me. I hugged her back and mischievously tugged at her hair again, just to let her know that everything was back to normal.

'So what about Edward?' I asked as we unhooked ourselves from each other.

'Oh, Edward,' she echoed, as if she'd just

remembered him. 'He's gone home to dry off.' I noticed the way Kate struggled to keep her lips from quivering. I felt my chin tremble in sympathy. Then the two of us simultaneously burst into loud, noisy laughter. A couple of stragglers from the younger classes wandered past us on their way out, staring at us as though we had recently escaped a lunatic asylum. 'Oh, we shouldn't laugh,' Kate said, wiping away the tears.

'No, we mustn't,' I agreed. Then we fell over each other as another bout of hysterics set in.

CHAPTER ELEVEN

I guess you could say things were different after that. Over the next few days a whisper could be seen going round the whole school, and by the end of the week I'd been transformed into Second Most Popular Girl (after my best friend, obviously). Following what was already being called my 'Dramatic Act of Bravery', people were virtually queuing up to speak to me, and one morning a shy first-former even asked for my autograph.

In fact, it all started to get too much for me. Most lunchtimes there'd be a straggly row of girls doing handstands against the school wall. Nikky and I were usually part of that untidy mess of legs. But by Friday lunchtime all the other girls had abandoned their handstand practice to watch me and Nikky.

'Keep it up,' grunted Nikky determinedly as her elbows wobbled with the strain. 'Don't let them put you off.'

But it was difficult keeping a handstand going when all you could see before you was an upside-down row of socks and shoes silently scrutinizing you. Adoration is all well and good – but you really need to concentrate when the blood is rushing to your head.

From my upside-down view of the world, I recognized a familiar set of scuffed trainers walking towards the cloakroom. I allowed my legs to fall back down to the ground, scattering kids as they avoided a foot in the eye. I pulled my clothes straight and went to follow Peter, leaving Nikky still upside down with her face turning from red to purple.

I let the cloakroom door swing shut behind me and let out a sigh of relief. Honestly, I was quickly beginning to realize what a burden it must be for Kate putting up with this kind of thing every day. I threw myself on a bench and waited.

'Whatcha doin'?' I asked the air in front of me casually. We hadn't had a chance to talk properly ever since I'd become Ms Wonderful at school. Peter poked his head out from his anorak. He wasn't actually *wearing* his anorak. He'd perched on one of the benches, pulling his knees up so he could hide behind the coat as it hung from one of the brass hooks. Slowly one leg and then another emerged as he stood up to come and sit on the bench opposite me. We sat in silence for a few minutes while we concentrated on staring each other out.

'Guess you're pretty sorted now, then?' Peter asked eventually, his eyelids barely flickering. My eyes were beginning to water and Peter swam hazily in front of me.

'Reckon so,' I replied, and watched him carefully because he looked as though he was going to sneeze. He wiggled his nose cautiously and then smiled as he conquered the tickle. Nikky appeared at the cloakroom windows making kissing actions, which made both of us blink involuntarily as we turned to look at her. I scowled at her and she wandered off. I turned my gaze back to Peter. 'But not completely sorted.'

'How's that?' Peter asked.

'Well, it's all well and good. But, I mean . . .'

'What?' he prompted.

'Well, it doesn't really mean anything, does it? Not when the one person you *want* to say well done is skulking in the cloakroom.'

Peter shrugged his shoulders.

'Come on. Be glad for me.'

'I am,' protested Peter. 'But it's hard to make myself heard with that rabble out there.'

'Well, why do you think I'm in here, then?' I replied. I waited but it didn't look as though Peter was going to say anything.

'Come on,' I said, grabbing him by the arm and yanking him up. 'Let's get out of here.' The end-of-lunch bell was ringing and Peter and I ran for the cloakroom door, tripping up over our own feet. I tried to drag him down the corridor, to stay ahead of all the other kids, but Peter pulled back and forced me to stop.

'Come *on*!' I screeched in frustration. I wanted to get to the safety of the classroom before any of those other kids started bothering me again.

'Hang on a minute,' he said, and I turned

round impatiently. Peter smiled. 'Well done,' he said eventually.

'Thanks,' I replied, unable to stop a grin escaping. And for the first time that day, I actually enjoyed the attention.

CHAPTER TWELVE

We were soon caught up in frantic last-minute practice for the play and before we knew it, Final Rehearsal had arrived. As I walked into the assembly hall you could smell the excitement in the air. I couldn't see the stage for the crush of kids gathered round it and even the teachers were hesitantly poking their noses out of the staffroom door to see what was going on. The dinner ladies had arrived early for their temporary promotion to the role of make-up artists. I wasn't sure how their skill with a meat and potato pie was going to help them with a mascara wand, but Mr Taylor seemed to think the two roles required similar skills.

Mrs McCabe, head of the dinner ladies, pushed past me with Delilah's wig and I caught sight of Kate. She was chatting to Edward, and I decided that now was the time to go over and make sure that everything was OK between Edward and me. He was the only person I hadn't really apologized to. But before I had chance to do anything Miss Cameron marched towards me with an armful of fake fur, caught me by the hand and led me into the library cum temporary changing room.

As I walked into the dressing room I was greeted by the sight of two familiar but clearly anxious girls from my year, standing in a big mess of fake fur and looking vaguely donkey-shaped. However, it was only when one of them reached up a hoof to scratch her nose that I realized that this travesty of sewing was what could be laughingly called a 'donkey costume'.

I looked back up at Miss Cameron, who was smiling broadly at me.

'You cannot be serious,' I said with deadly seriousness.

'It's not *so* bad,' said one of the donkeys, who I now recognized as Clare Joyce. But as she walked towards me my nose started to itch, and when she put a comforting furry arm round my shoulders a sneeze erupted. I tentatively felt my face to make sure my nose was still where it was meant to be.

'Oh dear,' said Miss Cameron faintly.

The other donkey started crying. 'I need to go to the toilet,' she complained plaintively.

The sneezing didn't stop. As Miss Cameron knelt on the floor and held the Third Donkey outfit open for me I reluctantly stepped into the two back legs of the costume. And sneezed loudly. The two of us struggled to force my arms into the two front legs, until another storm of sneezing forced both of us to stop.

'I'm not meant to do this,' I told my teacher as she struggled with the long zip that ran up the front of the costume. 'This is a health hazard,' I admonished her. 'I'll probably *die*.'

Miss Cameron was having none of it. She roughly shoved a bunch of tissues into my hand and steered me towards a mirror, grinning over my shoulder at our reflection.

'Oh, Emma, it's perfect.'

Cunning. But that wasn't going to wash. 'It's a mockery,' I replied.

'You're going to do so well out there,' she continued, ignoring me. 'Now don't look like that. Go on, show them what you're made of.'

And with that, she pushed me towards the library door and the assembly hall full of kids. Reluctantly, I dragged my feet (or should I say, hooves) towards the door. I knew what I was made of all right – three parts fake fur and one part embarrassment. But there was no escape now. It was time for the rest of the school to see the tackiest show of fake fur this side of Harvey Nichols.

As I stepped out into the assembly hall, I swear a hush descended. I saw people turning round one by one to look in my direction. I expected jeering at the very least, but for some reason, everyone seemed dead impressed. *Perhaps this outfit isn't so terrible after all,* I tried to reassure myself. As I continued watching the reaction, I could see the teachers crowd together animatedly. Peter was grinning from ear to ear and Nikky was nodding approvingly. Then Mr Taylor stepped forward, looking fit to burst, and held a hand out.

'Me?' I started to ask, pointing a hoof at my chest. Just as I began to reach out hesitantly to Mr Taylor's proffered arm, I felt something brush past me. I turned round just in time to watch Kate, with a serene smile on her face, hook her arm through Mr Taylor's. Behind her I could see Miss Cameron and Mrs McCabe huddled together and looking like they'd burst with pride. They'd done a good job on Kate, I had to admit. The Delilah wig suited her perfectly and Mrs McCabe had drawn thick, black lines of kohl round her eyes to give her that exotic Bible look. And you could be sure Kate's outfit wasn't made of dodgy fake fur – she wore a toga of shimmering gold.

Mortified, I waited for the ground to open up and swallow me. I shuffled my hooves impatiently, but nothing seemed to happen. OK, I was still feeling a bit – well – foolish, shall we say. But I looked at the floor beneath me and it was still there, all solid-looking.

Then, as the other kids oohed and aahed over Kate's costume, Edward jumped down from the stage and ran over to me excitedly, his Samson wig wobbling on his head.

'Come on, Emma. Up on stage with us.' I looked at him closely, keen to search out any sign of mockery. There was none, no matter how hard I looked.

As I hesitated, Mr Taylor turned round and beckoned to me. 'Come on, Emma. We need you up here.'

Edward grabbed hold of my hand, ceremoniously leading me towards the centre of the stage. I took my place next to my best friend, who was beaming excitedly at me and totally ruining the sophisticated Delilah look. It felt pretty good to be up there with everyone smiling and cheering us on.

I looked round at Edward before we all went backstage ready to begin the rehearsal. 'Thank you,' I said.

✩ ✩ ✩

The next morning, as the day of the opening performance arrived, I woke up at 5.30 a.m. and couldn't get back to sleep. I opened the bedroom curtains when I heard the milkman's float just in time to see him deliver the usual two pints to our doorstep. I switched my bedside lamp on and half-heartedly picked up a book. It was no good, I couldn't concentrate and after a few minutes I slipped out of bed and crept down the stairs.

Mum must have had her radar on because she followed me into the kitchen and gently pushed me towards the kitchen table. I perched on one of the chairs and watched as Mum rescued the milk bottles from outside, poured the contents of one into a pan and lit the hob. She sat down next to me, tucking her dressing gown tighter. We looked at each other and I swallowed nervously. She put her arm round my shoulders and pulled me towards her, burying her face in my hair.

'Don't worry, sweetness,' she said quietly. 'You're going to be a star.'

☆ ☆ ☆

I don't think any of us got much work done at school that day. We tried to have normal lessons in the morning, but nobody could concentrate and we were all really jumpy. From our classrooms, we could hear Mr Inglethorp hammering and singing as he made a few last-minute adjustments to the stage, and Mr Key's voice ringing out from his office, issuing terse instructions to the caretaker to be quiet.

Finally, after lunch, Mr Key called all the school together in the assembly hall. We nervously sat down cross-legged on the floor as our headmaster stepped up on to the stage.

'I've brought you all together for a few final words before tonight's performance of *Samson and Delilah*.' He paused, looking round at all the anxious faces watching him, and smiled. 'I know you've all worked very hard indeed getting this play ready, and I want to say how proud I am of my staff and pupils. In particular, I think we should all pay credit to one teacher who has selflessly given up many hours of his own time to bring this play together.' He beckoned to Mr Taylor.

Mr Taylor stepped up on to the stage and nervously walked over to Mr Key.

'Three cheers for Mr Taylor!' called out the headmaster. The assembly hall erupted in cheers and clapping. As I looked round the hall I noticed Mrs Rogers watching from behind one of the doors leading out into the corridor. She shook her head in disgust and turned away, rushing off when she caught sight of a first-former daring to run down the corridor.

Mr Taylor blushed and shoved his fists deep into his pockets, pulling his jacket all out of shape. He rubbed the stubble on his chin with the back of his hand and cleared his throat.

'Girls and boys. I am so very proud of you and I know you're going to make me even more proud by the end of tonight. But in the meantime . . . let's start getting ready!'

He clapped his hands together and we all jumped to our feet. Mr Key dived for cover back into his office as the whole school ran towards the stage.

☆ ☆ ☆

The rest of the day rushed by far too quickly as we tried to remember our lines for the final run-through, and struggled to keep the hysteria at bay. Mr Inglethorp slowly put out rows of chairs for the audience. This was the first time the chairs had been laid out and it was pretty frightening to see how many parents could be crammed into one assembly hall.

Far too quickly, we ran out of time and were herded into Miss Cameron's classroom to keep us out of the way while the parents arrived. We weren't allowed to peek, but the noise of grown-ups was filling the assembly hall and Nikky couldn't resist pushing the door open a few centimetres. As she did so, the smell of perfume all the mums had dabbed behind their ears hit us, and there was definitely more than a hint of aftershave floating around. These weren't the usual kinds of school smells. I sneezed and pulled my head back into the classroom.

Kate was over on the other side reading the script, her lips moving silently as she went through her lines. I retired to a quiet corner of the classroom and Peter came over to sit next to me. Though we didn't say much to each other, it just made me feel better to have him sitting there. He squeezed my arm and I squeezed his in return. That was all we needed to do.

Just then Mr Taylor leapt into the room. He was in a barely controlled frenzy of excitement.

'OK, everyone! All the parents are

here, so we're just about ready to start the play. Mr Key is going to give a small speech of introduction, then the lights will go down and I will come back here to give you your cue. Got that?'

Thirty frightened faces nodded silently. Mr Taylor backed out of the classroom, giving us an exaggerated thumbs up and shut the door behind him. We gathered round, ready to make our entrance. Kate and I put our arms round each other.

'Break a leg,' I whispered to her. She looked down at my costume.

'Yeah, and don't make an ass of yourself.'

I was just about to come back with something devastatingly witty, when the classroom door opened and in the darkness we heard a bang and 'Oof!' as Mr Taylor tripped over his own feet and fell to the floor. We crowded round him and looked at our teacher as he rubbed one of his knees.

'Go on, then!' he hissed. 'That's your cue.' Kate calmly stepped over him and led the way to the stage.

Samson and Delilah – the musical had started.

CHAPTER THIRTEEN

What can I say? Kate was brilliant. But you know what? So was everybody, including me. OK, so some of the 'hee-haws' got a bit loud at times, and I did have a bit of trouble with the occasional sneeze. But I just remembered what my mum told me about her first acting experience and everyone fluffing their lines – and I realized it didn't really matter that much. I could see Mum and Dad smiling proudly out in the audience and it felt good.

What was great was that everyone had someone sitting out in the audience cheering them on. As we took our final bow, parents and friends broke out of the rows of seats and hurried to the front of the stage. It was very interesting to see some of my schoolmates with their parents. I could see Dave Pilchard looking like butter wouldn't melt in his mouth with his mum and dad.

Nikky's dad was proud as Punch of her, but didn't quite seem to know how to show it. In the end, he gave her a mock right jab on the chin and mumbled, 'Attagirl,' before blowing loudly into his handkerchief.

Inevitably, my own mum grabbed the opportunity for a stint of amateur dramatics. 'Darling, it's the best donkey I've ever seen up on stage. Better even than Bottom in *A Midsummer Night's Dream!*'

High praise indeed.

But as I looked round the assembly hall, there was one person I couldn't see.

'Where's Peter?' I asked as I struggled out of Mum's grasp.

Dad shrugged his shoulders. 'I don't know where he is, love. His mum's over there.'

He pointed out Peter's mum, waiting by the door of the assembly hall. I ran over to her.

'Hello, Mrs Joy, where's Peter?'

'He's just changing and then we're off home, pet. I think he's in your classroom.'

'OK, thanks,' I said and walked over to the

classroom. I pushed the door open and peeked inside. Peter was just pulling his jumper over his head, and as his face emerged, hot and bothered, he spotted me. I stepped into the room.

'You found me, then?' he asked, as if he'd been expecting it.

'How did you know I'd be looking?'

'Well, you should have been. You've a lot to thank me for.'

I wasn't sure what to make of all this. Laid-back Peter seemed to have more and more to say for himself these days. He bent over to tie up his shoelaces, forcing me to wait until we could continue the conversation. When he stood again his face was flushed, but he was smiling.

'Like what?' I countered. I realized I was blushing and I had no idea why.

'For making sure you never had to be a Billy No Mates when you'd fallen out with Kate.'

I pulled at my ponytail nervously.

'For forcing you to make friends with Kate.'

I suddenly found that piece of chewing gum on the floor immensely interesting.

'And for generally being the nicest boy you could hope to have around.'

This was too much. 'Yes, well . . . really . . . I'm not sure that . . . I mean, I don't know what you're talking about,' I finished eloquently.

'Course you don't, Emma. But that's OK, I'm not going to extract an acknowledgement out of you.'

Damn, this boy was good.

'Anyway, I hope you like fish fingers.'

'Why?' I asked, confused by the sudden change of subject.

'Cos you're coming round to mine for your tea tomorrow night.'

SWALK

'You can't tell me what to do!' I exclaimed, trying to sound convincingly outraged.

Peter looked me straight in the face, with one eyebrow raised ironically. 'So let me get this straight. You're saying you would prefer to have tea made by your mum? No? OK, then. See you about five.'

And as I opened and closed my mouth, gulping like a fish, Peter calmly walked out of the classroom.

I was left standing on my own. I kicked the leg of my desk and swung my shoulders, trying to feel angry. But it was no good. You can't fake outrage, no matter how hard you try. Especially when what you're actually feeling is quietly thrilled.

As I looked out of the classroom door I could see Peter and his mum leaving the assembly hall. I waited to see if Peter would glance back. Just before the doors swung shut behind him, he turned round and met my gaze with a slow, lazy wink. I grinned back, letting out the breath that I hadn't even noticed I was holding.

I strode out of the classroom to find my mum, dad, baby brother and Kate all waiting for me. We were the last people left in the hall and the stage suddenly looked very big and lonely without any of us up on it.

'Ready to go home?' Kate asked. Mum and Dad hovered impatiently in the background, car keys jangling.

'As I'll ever be,' I replied, hooking my arm comfortably through my friend's.

'Did you find Peter?' Mum asked as we turned to go.

'Oh yes, I found him,' I said mysteriously. My parents looked quizzically at each other, but I didn't feel like explaining. For the time being at least, I wanted to keep my new, extra-special friendship with Peter a secret. Well, I mean. We all need to have something nice to keep to ourselves once in a while, don't we? I knew my best friend would agree with me on that one.

So there you have it. That was My Life as Third Donkey. In the end, and I hate to admit it, I actually enjoyed myself. Mr Taylor says next year he's thinking of doing *My Fair Lady*. No donkeys in that one. Mum's already enrolled me for singing lessons and if she had her way, I think she'd be taking part in the next play herself. Fortunately, Mr Taylor says strictly no parents allowed. Kate says she's not going to take part next time. But I've heard her singing to herself and I know she fancies the role of Eliza Doolittle. Me? Oh, just a small part will do. Nothing major. Honestly.